D/S Jack

Investigates

A
Double murder
In
Rhyl

By

dp jones

Chapter 1.

Five weeks, after being charged with multiple offences of murder and, despite the seemingly, incontrovertible evidence against him, former surgeon, Dr Eugene Glendenning was granted conditional bail.

Then, only days later, D/S Jack Czerniak, the investigating officer in the case, was summarily summoned, to the office, of Detective Chief Inspector Andrews.

"You wanted to see me boss?" Czerniak asked, as he entered the office, his arms filled, with a bundle of dusty, buff coloured sudden death files.

"Yes, come in Jack," Andrews replied, in an, almost absent-minded manner, before seeing the bundle of files, "what, the blood and thunder have you got there?"

"Oh, yeh, well," Czerniak replied, looking rather sheepishly, "listen boss, I know you told me to leave it to the CPS and our barrister but."

"But what?" Andrews said sharply, before Jack could finish his explanation, "that, as per usual, you thought, as everyone else was so incompetent, you would dig around in the bloody archives, hoping to unearth, previously undiscovered evidence against our doctor."

"Well, can you blame me, I mean, come on boss, you have to admit, that it's all been a bit too bloody cosy, between Glendenning's legal team and Harcourt," Czerniak replied angrily, "what are they, golfing buddies or something?".

"Christ almighty man, are you suggesting, that Assistant Commissioner Harcourt, has been passing vital information over to Glendenning's defence team and, on a bloody golf course of all places," DCI Andrews snapped back, "because if you are, then you're walking a very dangerous path and, I might add, alone."

"Bloody hell, is it just me," Jack said, as he dropped the bundle of files onto a chair, "I mean, how many other murderer suspects do you know, were let out on bail after they'd admitted, under caution and, in a taped interview, that they had deliberately poisoned several people."

"Granted, it is highly unusual but, not unprecedented," Andrews replied, his mood, now a lot calmer, "and, like his brief said, he was both contrite and devastated, by those horrific offences, which he now says, were carried out by Sister Ronnie Brooks, his one-time, trusted friend and colleague and, that when his trial commences, he intends to produce, irrefutable evidence, which shows, that Dr Glendenning, not only, played no part in those killings but, was tricked into making a confession, which of course, he now retracts and, vehemently denies."

"Bloody tricked, Christ almighty boss, his brief was in the room at the time and you and Harcourt were next door listening in," Czerniak said, his anger, now all too apparent.

"Come on Jack, you're taking it too personally, Christ you've been a copper long enough to know how these things work and, how barristers love to play mind games."

"So, he's going to walk away from a string of murders and do what," Jack asked, his arms raised in despair, "go back to drugging, another long line of poor homeless alcoholics, just so he can get himself a knighthood, for all his, so-called, good works."

"Look, you've done your best and, no one can say you didn't go over and above what any normal copper would have done, so, let it go, do you hear me, let it go, and that mister, is a bloody order."

"From you, or above," Jack asked quietly.

"Jesus Christ, you really are a royal pain in the arse at times."

"Yeh, well, I hate to see injustice at any level," Jack said, as he bent down to pick up the bundle of files, "oh by the way, what was it you wanted to see me about?"

"Christ, yes I almost forgot," Andrews replied, as he searched for a folder, on his over cluttered desk, "yes, sit down there a minute and tell me, how well do you know Wales?"

"Bloody Wales, what is this, some sort of geography test?" Czerniak replied, as he ignored his boss and turned to leave the office.

"Jesus Christ Jack, do you make a point, of being so bloody awkward with everything, now get over here and sit down for god's sake."

"I'm sorry boss, but it's you, you're being so abstract, I mean, what sort of question is that to ask anyone, how well do you know bloody Wales."

"Well, let's make it easier for you shall we, have you ever been to Wales?"

"Yes, when I was a kid, my dad took us to Rhyl for a week and, as it rained, every bloody day," he replied with a slight chuckle, "I hated every sodden minute of it, why do you ask."

"Well, funny you should mention Rhyl, because the local force, that covers that charming, little seaside resort, is dealing with a double murder and, we've been asked to assist."

"Assist, that's a bit 'Fabian of the Yard' isn't it, I mean, I thought outside forces stopped asking for the Mets assistance, what, well over fifty years ago."

"Yes, well under normal circumstances, they would have dealt with it in-house but, seeing as the main suspect is one of their own, the home office, want a completely independent team on it."

"One of their own, do you mean, they've arrested a copper for it?"

"Not exactly no, seems, he was found at the scene and, as one of the victims was his estranged wife and the other, her boyfriend, it puts him in the frame, as number one suspect."

"So why hasn't he been arrested?"

"Well, for one thing, he's a Superintendent and another, he's got a water tight alibi."

"And what, because I'm ruffling far too many feathers here, I'm being farmed out to the sticks, to deal with a domestic murder enquiry."

"No, the home office wanted a team of experienced murder squad detectives and, in light of your recent success with Dr Glendenning and Ronnie Brooks, they personally asked for you and your team," he replied, before pushing another document across his desk towards Czerniak, "and, as you can see, in light of that, they've authorised funding, for a Detective Inspector and a couple of sergeants to investigate the case."

"So, whose going with us?"

"No one, you numpty because, for the duration, you'll be an acting D/I and, Tony Smith and Rajni, as they've both passed their sergeants exam, will each, be an acting D/S."

"That's something I suppose."

"Something, it's more than something, it's a step up the bloody ladder man," Andrews said, a little annoyed that Czerniak wasn't more grateful.

"And what, you now want us to drop everything we're currently doing, pack a bucket and spade and head over to sunny Rhyl."

"Well, from what I can see, you've got nothing pressing at the moment and, as it's April already, I'm sure it won't rain, well, not every day anyway," Andrews said with a broad grin, "oh, and Jack, before you go, take that lot downstairs and bury them, back in the bloody archives."

Despite feeling, that somewhere behind the scenes, Assistant Commissioner Harcourt was manipulating the strings, Jack reluctantly stepped into the lift and, descended four floors, to the basement.

However, instead of returning the sudden death files, directly to the archivist, he went into an empty office and there, spent the next hour, scanning through them.

There were seventy-three files in total and, had been specifically chosen, because each of them, related to former patients of the Royal

Alexander Hospital, whose deaths, had been sudden and, unexplained.

Some of the files, only contained one sheet of A4 paper and, as they only gave very brief details of the patient's symptoms and, possible cause of death, they were of no evidential value and so, Czerniak, quickly put them to one side.

Of the remaining, forty-two files, five of the patients had spent time, in the hospitals neurological ward and two, had been treated for their addiction to alcohol, in the clinic, established by Glendenning.

As it was quite feasibly, that all seven patients could have come into contact with Dr Glendenning and, or, Sister Ronnie Brooks, Jack stuffed their files inside his jacket.

Having personally returned, the remaining sixty-six files to Gerry Barlow, the archivist, Czerniak made a point of expressing, at some length, his dismay, at not discovering any new evidence against Dr Glendenning.

Knowing, that the archivist, was a renowned gossip and, source of many a rumour which had circulated around the force, Jack headed for the lift, happy in the knowledge, that his supposed failure to find any new evidence, would quickly filter back to Assistant Commissioner Harcourt.

"Okay, listen up you lot," Czerniak said loudly, above the chatter in the general office, "I've got some good news, well, for two of you anyway, firstly, the DCI, in his infinite wisdom, has asked me, to take you all away on holiday."

"Bloody hell sarge," DC Tony smith yelled, from the far side of the room, "call that good news, why, where are you taking us, Southend on Sea or, hop picking in Kent."

With laughter erupting all around the office, Czerniak was finding it hard to make himself heard and so, he stood on a chair.

"Okay, okay, calm down," he yelled loudly, "Christ, you're like a bunch of bloody kids, so, no, we're not going hop picking, we are in fact, going all the way to Welsh Wales, to help solve a case."

"Bloody Wales, what's happened sarge, has someone stolen some sheep or something," DC Danny Murphy called out, sounding most disappointed.

"No, apparently, the Home Office wants us to look into a double murder."

"Why us sarge?" DC Rajni Latifa asked, sounding as disappointed as DC Murphy, "I mean, I know there all a bit backward up there, but surely, the locals can handle a job like that, can't they?"

"That's what I said but, it seems, the main suspect is a serving officer and, not only was he first on the scene but, after calling it in, he tried to revive the victims, by giving CPR," Czerniak replied, as he climbed down from the chair.

"Shit, that's a little bit too pat isn't it," Rajni said, after hearing that bit of information, "because now, any forensic evidence or DNA found on the bodies and linked to him, will have to be automatically discounted."

"Yeh, and, what makes it even more intriguing, the two victims, were his estranged wife and, her new boyfriend."

"Christ sarge, he's obviously guilty, so why the hell have we been called in to pick up the pieces?" Tony Smith asked.

"Well, on the face of it, it certainly sounds like he is, but the thing is, as our main suspect is a Superintendent Griffiths who, I'm told, was allegedly at a function, in the local golf club and, enjoying a drink, with numerous other coppers, when the killings took place."

"So, what you're saying in effect, is that despite everything pointing to him, our main suspect, has a cast-iron alibi," DC Smith said, now far more subdued.

"Sounds like it, yes," Czerniak replied.

"Shit, is there any other good news," DC Smith asked.

"Oh yes, and believe me, it gets better and better," Czerniak replied, handing DC Smith the file he'd been given by DCI Andrews, "as it seems, our Superintendent, who only lives a few minutes' walk from the golf club, chose to leave the function at one o'clock in the morning and, instead of going home, drove about ten miles or so to Rhyl and the house, where his estranged wife, was living with her boyfriend."

"Says here," DC Smith said, reading an extract from the file, "that he apparently found the front door open and walked in, to find them both dead."

"So why contaminate the scene any further and, why give CPR?" Danny Murphy asked, "I mean, he's a bloody Superintendent for god's sake, Christ, you wouldn't expect your bog - standard wooden top, do something like that."

"That my friends, is what we need to find out, so, go home, pack a bag and be back here within the hour."

"Hang on a minute sarge, you said just now, that you had good news for two of us," Rajni said, as she picked up her coat.

"Oh yeh, sorry, nearly forgot," he replied awkwardly, "look, there's no way of saying this, without disappointing you Danny but, for the duration of the enquiry, Tony and Rajni will be acting sergeants."

"That's okay sarge, maybe if I'd have knuckled down and studied a bit more."

"Yeh, well, with a young family, it's always going to be difficult," Czerniak said, trying to console, the youngest member of the team.

"Cheers sarge," he replied, looking somewhat deflated, "but congratulations you two and, before you start to get any big ideas, above your station, you can make your own tea."

"How is that going to work then?" Rajni suddenly said, "as we can't have three sergeants, I mean, who's going to make all the decisions?"

"Me," Czerniak replied, "as I've been made acting D/I."

"Bloody hell, well done sarge, sorry, I mean boss," Tony Smith said.

"Well, thank you very much, Detective Sergeant Smith."

"Hmm, yeh, got a bit of a ring to it," Tony Smith said, "and, I can't wait to use it when I answer the phone, what about you Rajni?"

"Hmm, yes, I think my father will be proud," she replied, with a rather modest smile, as she left the office.

Chapter 2.

"Bloody hell sarge, sorry, boss, I thought you said, this place, was called sunny Rhyl," acting, Detective Sergeant Tony Smith complained, as he ran into the hotel foyer from a rain spattered carpark.

"Christ Tony, it's only a slight, April shower," Czerniak said, with a chuckle, "you wait, until it really starts raining, then you'll have something to complain about."

"And just look at my new suede boots, they're ruined," Tony groaned, as he tried to wipe off, the mud splatters, with a piece of tissue.

"Right, when you've finished giving your hello and, welcome to Wales speech, perhaps you can go and book us in," Czerniak said, handing Tony Smith his holdall, "as I've got to go and find St Asaph and, our local liaison officer."

"Do you need to borrow my phrase book boss," Rajni asked, as Czerniak was exiting the hotel.

"No need sergeant, I can already do my bora da and diolchs," he replied, as he let the door close behind him, "see you later."

The small, family run hotel, on the edge of Rhuddlan, was only a ten-minute car journey from the sub divisional police headquarters at St Asaph, but the road, Czerniak had chosen to use that afternoon, was both narrow and winding and, combined with the driving rain, it had become appalling.

"So, you found us alright then," D/I Mel Jones said, with an outstretched hand.

"Yeh no problem, though that back road from Rhuddlan was a bit of a nightmare in this rain."

"Bloody hell, no one uses that road, well, not unless they've had a drink and want to avoid getting caught by the traffic department," he said, tapping the side of his nose, "right, come through and I'll show you around."

After a brief tour of the building, D/I Jones took Czerniak up to the second floor and, into a large open plan office, containing five desks and accompanying chairs and very little else.

"You and your team have been allocated this room," he said, walking over to the window, "as you can see, it has a marvellous view of the mountains but, more importantly, no bugger can see in, so, providing you keep the door locked at all times, you should have sufficient privacy."

"Who else knows why we're here?" Czerniak asked, as he gazed out of the window at a very soggy landscape.

"Practically everyone I should imagine, as you can't keep something like this a secret, well, not in such a small force like ours," he replied, with a faint smile.

"And, what is the general feeling, in the force, especially in the local C.I.D?"

"Pretty much as you would expect, as on one hand, you've got those who believe it should have been dealt with in-house and on the other, well, to be perfectly honest with you, I don't think I've heard anyone say they think it's a good idea, you know, bringing in an outside team, especially from the Met, no offence."

"None taken," Czerniak replied, before asking, "so, are we likely to meet any hostility locally?"

"I hope not, but if you do, let me know immediately so I can nip it in the bud," he said, before taking a seat at one of the five empty desks, "now then, what do you need to know about the job?"

"Well, I know the bodies were found during the early hours of last Saturday morning, which was what, the fifteenth of April," Czerniak replied, as he too, took a seat, "and erm, that one of the victims was the estranged wife of a serving officer, but apart from that, not much else, so perhaps we could start with the basic who, where and when and of course, if you know, why it happened."

"So, the bodies of Linda Griffiths and Garry Sunderland were, as you say, discovered just after 1.30am last Saturday morning," he replied, shifting awkwardly in his seat, "by erm, Superintendent John Griffiths who, as you already know, was estranged from his wife."

"And both had been shot, is that right?" Czerniak asked.

"Erm, yes, that's correct," DI Jones replied, "Mrs Griffiths was shot three times and, Mr Sunderland once, erm, in the, erm head."

"How long, had Superintendent Griffiths and his wife been separated?"

"From what I can gather, they had been living apart for the past five weeks."

"And, was she living full time with this, Mr Sunderland?"

"As far as I know yes, seems they met, when John, erm, sorry, Superintendent Griffiths, purchased a car from the garage, run by Garry Sunderland."

"How long ago was that?"

"Again, as you can imagine at this early stage, things are a little sketchy," he replied with a faint, awkward smile, "but I believe, it was about six months ago, maybe a bit longer, I'm not too sure."

"From what I could glean, from the preliminary file, the Home Office sent, Mrs Griffiths was a lot younger than her husband, had they been married long?"

"Three years," he replied, as once again he shifted awkwardly in his seat, "look, I might as well tell you, rather than you hearing it third hand from some gossip and, well, long before she met John, she had a bit of a reputation, you know, for playing the field."

"How did they meet?"

"Erm, well, for nearly twelve months, after erm, Mary, John's first wife, died of cancer, he became something of a loner and, I have to admit, a concern for many of us."

"In what way."

"Well, to be perfectly blunt, one or two of us, expressed real concerns, about him, you know, being a suicide risk but then, out of the blue, he started playing golf again."

"Is that how they met?"

"Sorry, no, well, not directly no," D/I Jones replied, "you see, like most forces, we have golfing teams, you know, who play, sort of, erm, interdivisional matches and that sort of thing."

"Yes, I get the picture."

"Anyway, with golf, then taking up the majority of his free time, John joined the B division team and, I think it's fair to say, acquitted himself admirably on several occasions," he said, with a faint smile, "and, from what I can gather from various sources, it was, whilst playing in a competition against C division, that he met Linda."

"Was she a police officer as well?"

"No, she worked in C division's admin office, which is in Prestatyn," he replied with a slight sigh, "and, if the rumour machine is to be believed, whilst she was working there, was the cause of one or two relationships breaking up."

"So, was she playing that day?"

"Well, if she was, it certainly wasn't golf," he replied, with a certain amount of anger in his voice.

"Do I take it, that you didn't much like her?"

"Look, I wasn't there on the day, but by all accounts, she homed in on John, like some bloody Exocet guided missile and, from the moment he returned to the club house after his game, she was apparently, all over him like a rash."

"So, what was the age difference when they met?"

"Erm John, was I believe, forty-five and she, had just turned thirty."

"Was she attractive?"

"I think the expression, is voluptuous," he replied awkwardly.

"Bloody hell Mel, that's a bit of a Victorian way of describing someone," Czerniak said, with a slight chuckle, in the hope he could get D/I Jones to relax.

"Look, I don't know what it's like up in the Met, but here, the bloody politically correct brigade is hiding around every corner and, well."

"Well nothing, let me tell you, they aren't coming in here, so go on, If I'm to get a real feel for this case, I need to know, what she was like."

"Hmm, yes, well, she was attractive with long dark hair and you know, a slim waist and, a fuller figure, in erm, in all the right places and, or so I'm told, used her attributes to get whatever she wanted," he replied, nervously wringing his hands.

"So, did John Griffiths know of her past reputation?"

"Huh, erm, well, if he did, he certainly turned a blind eye to it."

"And, how long after this initial meeting did they get married?"

"Not long, six months or so."

"So, something of a whirlwind romance?"

"Yes, you could say so, but unfortunately, it was destined to failure from the outset because, and again, I must stress these are just rumours, which have erm, only come to light since her death, but, I think she was erm, seeing another man, a former boyfriend apparently."

"Was he also in the job?" Czerniak asked.

"No, I think he was a part time doorman, at one of the nightclubs in Rhyl."

"And John, would he have been aware of that relationship?"

"Yet again, if he was, he never shared his suspicions with anyone."

"So, what can you tell me about Garry Sunderland?"

"Without wishing to typecast anyone, he was, what you might call, your typical used car salesman, you know, swarthy complexion, with slicked back hair and all the patter," DI Jones replied, seemingly happier to be discussing someone else, other than Mrs Griffiths.

"What sort of cars did he sell?"

"Hmm, mostly sports cars, so as you can imagine, Linda's head would have been turned the moment they entered the showrooms."

"Was he married?"

"Divorced, about two years ago I believe, with an ex-wife and daughter, now living in Chester."

"You have been referring to Superintendent Griffiths as John, so, would I be correct in saying, you and he, are good friends?"

"Hmm, where do I begin," he said, with a rather awkward smile and, once again, nervously wringing his hands together, "yes, I like to think we are because, he's generally well liked and respected by most of us, very possibly, because he's one of us, you know, came up through the ranks."

"So, has he spent his entire career, solely in this force?"

"Yes, joined as a cadet, five years or so in uniform, then C.I.D. for a while before being promoted to sergeant and, if my memory serves me well, had a spell in the training department, before moving to Abergele as D/I then, Llandudno, as uniform Chief inspector, which is where we first met."

"Were you also in uniform?"

"No, I was a D/C at the time."

"So, how did you become friends?"

"Both in police accommodation, living next door to each other and our wives became friends, and from there, it was a natural progression, you know, going for a pint, having them around for dinner, that sort of thing."

"So, it must have hit you hard as well, when his first wife died."

"Well, not to put too fine a point on it, we were all devastated, mostly because she was so young."

Chapter 3.

"So, what have we got then boss?" Rajni asked, as the four of them ate dinner that evening.

"Well, for one thing, D/I Mel Jones, our liaison, may be a real gent, but he's far too close to our main suspect so, just be careful what you say in front of him."

"And speaking of Superintendent Griffiths, can we speak to him, or will we need someone of the same rank with us," DC Danny Murphy asked, as he finished his main course.

"Good question Danny and, as far as I know, as long as we treat him as a witness, we can interview him as such, which is why, Rajni and I are seeing him at 10.00am tomorrow."

With dinner over and, one or two lies, about wanting an early night and a clear head for the following morning, Czerniak bid everyone goodnight and headed off to his room.

Having double checked, the door was locked, Czerniak poured himself a generous glass of whisky and then, began perusing the first, of the seven, sudden death files he'd kept back from the Met archives.

Malcolm Saunders was a 58year old alcoholic and, one of the first patients to attend the rehab clinic, set up in the Royal Alexander Hospital, by Dr Glendenning.

Having been referred there, by a drop-in centre, based in Kings Cross, Mr Saunders had been on a course of Antabuse and, despite one or two early setbacks, when he'd relapsed into his old ways, he seemed, according to his file, to be making some progress.

With him being one of the first patients to attend the clinic, Malcolm was seen on several occasions by Dr Glendenning but, other than the course of Antabuse he'd been prescribed, the notes made no mention of any other medication.

This was, very much the case, with all but one of the other six patients and he, only differed from the others, because he was never treated personally by the surgeon.

Annoyed and frustrated, by what he saw, as yet another dead end, Czerniak tossed the files onto the small table in the corner of his room and went to bed.

The following morning, all four were up early and, after finishing breakfast, they were about to head off for St Asaph, when Czerniak received a phone call from DCI Andrews.

"What was the last thing I said to you, before you left my office," Andrews hissed down the phone.

"That it wouldn't be raining in Rhyl," Czerniak replied sarcastically.

"No, you cheeky bastard," Andrews said angrily, "about those bloody sudden death files."

"Take them back to the archives, which I did."

"All of them?"

"What, yes all of them," Czerniak snapped back, "Oh, I get it, a file has gone missing and, because I was down there it must have been me that took it."

"Listen mister, I've known you for far too bloody long, so don't sodding well lie to me, did you return all those files?"

"Christ boss, as far as I know, yes, I returned all, of those files."

"What is that supposed to mean?" Andrews demanded angrily.

"That I went down to the archives and, handed a bundle of files to Gerry Barlow."

"How many exactly?"

"Bloody hell boss, how am I supposed to know that, I mean, you saw them," Czerniak replied, feigning disbelief that his boss was questioning his integrity, "what was it, about fifty or so, maybe a few more?"

"Are you saying, you have no idea how many files you took out in the first place?"

"Look boss, I went down there and mooched around for about an hour or so, just pulling out the odd file randomly."

"Did you sign them out?"

"Erm no, no, that's right, Gerry had already gone for his lunch," Czerniak replied, before pausing to throw his room keys to Rajni, so that she could go and pick up his briefcase. "Hang on a minute boss, just thinking about it, there might be a faint possibility, that I may have put some of the files back in the wrong boxes."

"What?"

"Erm yeh, well, at the time I didn't really know what I was looking for and, like I said, I was picking out files at random and, you know, might have put one or two back in the wrong box," he said tongue in cheek, "why, how many are missing?"

"Seven in total," Andrews replied now somewhat calmer, "don't suppose, you've any idea which boxes you looked in?"

"Sorry boss, I was just opening boxes and randomly looking for any sudden deaths connected to the Royal Alex and Glendenning," he lied, "erm, look, will you tell Gerry I'm really sorry, I just didn't think."

As they left the hotel and a ray of sunlight, broke through an otherwise leaden sky, Rajni asked Czerniak if everything was okay.

"What, oh yeh, just Andrews bending my shell like, over some missing files," he replied as they climbed into the car, "I take it, the other two have already left for the murder scene."

"Yeh, they're meeting D/I Jones there in twenty minutes," she said, deep in thought, before asking him, "what is Mel short for boss?"

"What is what?" he asked, whilst trying to negotiate his way out of the hotel carpark.

"Mel, what is it short for?"

"Christ, here we go again," he said, as he strained his neck, to see if there was any oncoming traffic before emerging out of the narrow, carpark entrance, "don't tell me, you've been thinking about this all night and now, you believe, he's our killer."

"No, well, not all night and, erm unless you know something I don't, not the killer," she replied with a slight chuckle, "no, what I mean, is, he's got rather an odd name, you know for a fella."

"What, and yours and mine aren't, Christ Rajni, he's bloody Welsh," he laughed, "so he's bound to have an odd name, because up here, they nearly all speak a different language to you and me."

"God yeh, I never thought about that," she said, once again deep in thought, "so, what you're saying, is I could be in a room, where everyone is talking about me and I wouldn't know."

"Yeh, but that's normal for you though isn't it?" he said before laughing out aloud.

"Huh, cheers, and I love you too?" she replied, before joining in the laughter.

Built, sometime around 2002, the sub divisional headquarters at St Asaph housed, not only a plethora of admin staff, but the traffic department, dog section and local C.I.D. and, as they pulled into the enclosed carpark, at the rear of the building, they were watched, by several detectives.

"What do you think boss, is that our welcoming committee?" Rajni asked, as she stared back at the three detectives, who were leaning against an unmarked car.

"I'd say the opposite wouldn't you," Czerniak replied, as he saw the scowl on their faces.

"But surely, they must know why we're here."

"Yeh, but, we are, after all, potentially looking at one of their own," Czerniak replied as he pulled into a vacant parking bay.

Then, a few minutes later, as they walked the narrow gauntlet, between the three detectives and a line of parked cars, Rajni was tempted to turn and say something, but a nudge and, a knowing look from Czerniak told her to keep quiet.

"Listen, put yourself in their position, and ask yourself, how would you feel, if this was

Kennington and they were here to interview Andrews about his wife's murder," Czerniak said, as they travelled to the second floor in the lift.

"Point taken," she mumbled, as the lift doors hissed open.

For the next hour and a half, Czerniak and acting Detective Sergeant Rajni Latifa, worked tirelessly, turning the sparsely furnished office, into a working incident room.

Not wanting to be part of the local police, Intranet, Czerniak had brought four, of their own laptop computers from London and, although they could link them, into their hosts intelligence system, no one, he hoped, could view what they were inputting.

Then, once the set up was complete and, using, one of those laptops, Rajni began to gather, as much information as she could, on the shootings.

"There's not much to go on," she said, after trawling the on-line incident log, relating to the two deaths, "and, it seems, that it was some Chief Super in professional standards, who pulled the plug on the enquiry."

"When?" Czerniak asked, as he walked over to her desk.

"Erm, judging by what little there is on here, I'd say, about an hour or so after the bodies were found."

"So, that means, nothing has been done, no house to house enquiries and very definitely, no bloody statements taken," he said, looking over her shoulder, "bloody hell, talk about the first few hours being crucial, Christ almighty, four days have gone by and not one, not one sodding witness has been spoken to."

"Do you want me to get in touch with professional standards, to ask them, why nothing has been done?"

"No, I'll do that, you crack on and see if there's any intel on either of the victims," he replied, picking up the telephone.

"Professional standards, Chief Inspector Charleston speaking," a rather laconic voice said on the other end of the phone line.

"Hello Chief Inspector, DI Czerniak here, I don't know if you are aware but," he started to say.

"Let me stop you there acting Inspector," the Chief Inspector said, cutting across Czerniak and, emphasising that he knew his rank was only temporary, "yes, I'm fully aware of who you are and, more to the point, that you, and your three colleagues, have been called, to investigate an incident within our force boundaries, though, the whys and the where's of it are beyond me, as we are perfectly capable of conducting our own enquiries into such matters."

"Yes, Chief Inspector, I don't doubt that for one minute but, as you know, the Home Office decided otherwise," Czerniak countered strongly, whilst trying and failing, to sound both sympathetic and neutral on the matter, "but, the truth of the matter is, we are here and, we have a job to do, so, can I ask, why your department, put a stop, on any form of initial enquiries into the murders, being carried out?"

"I beg your pardon," he replied indignantly.

"I'm asking, why have none of the basic, initial enquiries been carried out," Czerniak said, now any thought of politeness gone out of his head, "I mean, here we are on day four and, not one statement has been taken and, from what I can gather, no one has gone from door to door asking questions."

"Are you questioning our ability as police officers?" he replied angrily.

"No sir, I'm asking, why no one has even bothered to ask the neighbours of the deceased, if they heard anything or, why none of the local CCTV has been checked for possible offenders, you know, basic policing," Czerniak said, his impatience, giving way to temper and utter frustration.

"That, acting Inspector Czerniak, is something you will have to take up with Chief Superintendent Cooke, so, unless you have any other queries, I'll bid you good day."

After throwing his phone across the desk, Czerniak got to his feet and, having kicked over a chair, he stormed out of the incident room.

Chapter 4.

With his, curly black hair, now greying on both sides and his eyes, heavy and bloodshot, Superintendent John Griffiths looked tired and worn out.

"Thank you for agreeing to see us at such short notice sir and, on behalf of my team and, myself, of course, I'd like to offer you our deepest sympathy," Czerniak began, after offering the superintendent a seat, "would you like a coffee or something before we start?"

"No, I'm fine thank you," he replied, his right-hand twitching on his lap, "I'd just like to get on, with whatever it is you need from me, so I can get away, from all of these suspicious looks."

For the next half hour, whilst Rajni took notes, Czerniak, whose temper had long since subsided, asked the superintendent, about how he'd met his wife and, about their relationship and, in the main, he replied very candidly.

However, when asked about his wife's relationship, with used car salesman, Garry Sunderland, the Superintendents twitching right hand, turned into a fist and his answers, far more guarded.

As a surprise birthday gift, he told them through clenched teeth, he had decided to buy his wife a sports car and, having found a bright red Mazda MX5 for sale, on Sunderland's forecourt, he had taken Linda to view it.

He also said, that almost from the moment they met, Sunderland began fawning all over his wife and, despite there being no problem with the vehicle, he'd telephoned their house on numerous occasions, to enquire if it was still running well.

Things came to a head, he told Czerniak, about three weeks after they'd purchased the car, when he found Sunderland, talking to his wife, on their driveway.

"Yes, I lost my temper with him," he said quite bluntly, "and, make of it what you will, because embarrassingly, it was witnessed at the time, by several of our friends and neighbours, I actually frog marched him down the drive and off our property and then, in extremely plain language, told him, never to return."

"So, would it be fair to say, that there was no love, lost between the two of you?" Czerniak asked.

"Listen, I know it's considered to be impolite, you know, to speak unkindly of the dead, but that man, was nothing more than a conniving and manipulating slime ball, who somehow thought, by worming his way into Linda's affections, he could get rich quick," he replied, now, with both fists clenched tightly and one of them, thumping his right leg.

"I take it, you mean, that if your wife divorced you, he would somehow get his hands on half your money."

"Exactly, which, I think I should point out, before you hear from some other source, is quite a considerable amount," he said quietly, "you see, Mary, my first wife, came from farming stock and, as she was, an only child, inherited the family farm when her parents died."

"But you don't run the farm now do you?"

"No, that's the point, you see, Mary was in the process of completing the sale, for nearly three million pounds, when she received her cancer diagnosis," he said with a sad shrug, "ironic really, when you think about it because, if we'd have found out sooner, she could have gone private and maybe, just maybe, survived that awful death."

"I am truly sorry for your loss," Czerniak said, whilst reaching out and placing a comforting hand on the superintendent's shoulder.

"Hmm, yes, thank you," he said, fighting back the tears, "so you can see why, I was determined to ensure, that Garry bloody Sunderland, didn't get his hands, on any of Mary's inheritance."

"I take it, the fact that your wife inherited so much money, was common knowledge within the force."

"Erm, yes, yes I suppose it was, as a number of my colleagues, had speculated at the time, whether or not I would pack the job in and become a gentleman farmer."

"Had that been a possibility?"

"Hmm, we'd talked about it, even thought about keeping the farm and running it, but it was out of the question, because for one thing, I didn't know one end of a cow from another, then, when Mary became ill and went downhill so fast," he said, before pausing to think for a few moments.

"Did she suffer for long?"

"No, thank god, no, from the initial diagnosis, to her funeral was almost six months to the day," he replied, again pausing to reflect, "after which, well, we had no children and, no family to speak of, so, I just threw myself into the job then, when my current post was advertised, I sat the board and was promoted."

"To deputy commander of the sub division."

"Yes, but out here in the sticks, we don't use the term commander, it's just, superintendent."

"Yes, point taken, so, when did you first discover, that Linda was seeing Garry Sunderland?" Czerniak asked, whilst quickly skirting around the fact, that Superintendent Griffiths, had already supplied, a clear motive, for wanting both his wife and the car dealer dead.

"I think, it was about a week or so after that fracas on our driveway, and apparently, as she felt it was incumbent on her to go and apologise for my behaviour and so, as she put it, once she got to his showrooms, one thing lead to another and, before she knew where she was, they were having sex on his desk," he replied, while once again holding back the tears, "and, as I was too blind or, just too stupid to see, what was going on right under my nose, I let him steal her away from me and now, well, what's the point in anything, I mean, I've lost everything haven't I."

"I'm told, that last Friday night, you were attending a function at Abergele golf club, is that right?" Czerniak asked, trying to change the subject slightly.

"Yes, erm Mel Jones, a good friend of mine, twisted my arm and invited me to the do, otherwise I'd have spent yet another night alone, staring at four square walls," he replied, quietly, whilst so obviously, dwelling on his previous remarks.

"Is that, Detective Inspector, Mel Jones?" Czerniak asked sharply, trying to get the Superintendent to focus on the questions.

"Erm, yes, yes of course, you will have met him already, isn't he acting as your liaison or something," he replied, now following the flow of the conversation again.

"What was the function in aid of?'

"Oh, erm, celebrating the election of the new female captain I think," he replied quietly.

"And, what time did you arrive at the golf club?"

"Oh, sometime around eight or, eight fifteen I believe."

"Did you sit with anyone in particular?"

"Well yes, as Mel had invited me I sat with him and Jill, his wife and another couple, Geraint and Julia Edwards, I think he's a retired draughtsman or something similar."

"And you left when?"

"Hmm, yes, let me see, yes, I think it was just before one o'clock, you know, on the Saturday morning."

"And, did you arrive and leave the golf club alone in your car?"

"Yes and, before you ask, no I hadn't been drinking because, since Linda left me, I've been taking rather strong sleeping tablets, which don't altogether agree with alcohol."

"So, you were sober, when you drove away from the golf club?" Czerniak asked, to confirm the point.

"Yes, so now, you'll be wanting to know, if I was sober, why did I drive into Rhyl and not directly home, to my house in Abergele."

"Well, being as you brought it up sir, perhaps you can explain your actions that morning and of course, the reasoning behind them."

"I only wish I could, I mean, I live less than a five minutes' walk from the golf club and, when I left, I fully intended going home but, after seeing so many happy couples enjoying themselves that night, I just thought," he said before stopping mid-sentence.

"You just thought what sir?"

"Oh, I don't know, that I might be able to persuade Linda, that he was only after the money and that, as sure as eggs are eggs, he would leave her once he'd got his hands on it."

"So, did you manage to speak with her?" Czerniak asked, not knowing, at that time, exactly when, Linda Griffiths and Garry Sunderland, had been shot dead.

"Well, no, obviously not, because she was dead, they both were," he said angrily.

"Can you tell me, why you went inside the house?"

"Well, as I pulled up outside their house, I could see there were lights on in the hallway and, as the front door was wide open, I thought there might have been a problem and so, without thinking," he said, before pausing to wipe the tears away from his eyes with the back of his hand, "I, erm, I went through the front door, and saw him, you know, Gary Sunderland, erm, lying at the bottom of the stairs, and erm, covered in blood."

"Was he still breathing?"

"Erm, well, to be perfectly honest with you Inspector, at that time, I was more concerned about Linda and so, I called her name several times then, when I went into the kitchen, I found her on the floor," he replied, bringing his hand up to his mouth to stifle, the automatic sound of grief coming from his throat.

"Did you realise at the time that both of them had been shot?"

"Erm, no, no not really, I mean, yes there was an awful lot of blood, but I just thought there had been some sort of terrible accident or, that they'd argued or something," he said, no longer trying to stem the flow of tears, "in fact, even when I was trying to give her mouth to mouth, I had no idea she'd been shot."

"What about Sunderland, did you try to revive him at all?"

"Erm yes, well, after realising that Linda, was already dead, I telephoned the emergency services and, I'm afraid to say," he replied, before pausing a moment, "erm, it was only when the operator, you know, as they do, asked if he erm, erm showed any signs of life, that I actually went to check for a pulse."

"And?"

"And, well, as I thought, I erm, felt a faint pulse on his neck, I began chest compressions and, I was still doing them when the ambulance crew arrived."

"I suppose, the obvious question to ask, is can you think of any reason why anyone would want to harm either of them?"

"Well, from what I'd found out about Garry Sunderland and his womanising, I suppose, you could take your pick from any number of disgruntled husbands, who would have gladly given him a good going over, but as for actually killing him, I mean, shooting him in the head like that, it has to have been some sort of professional hit, don't you think, I mean, it's so cold and clinical."

"Yes, I agree, so, do you know, if Sunderland was linked in anyway, to any organised crime groups or, maybe, local drug dealers?"

"Not that I know of, no, but that doesn't mean he wasn't, I mean, who knows what circles he moved in."

"Yes, I understand that but, with you suggesting, it was a hitman of some sort, who killed both of them, I thought you were implying, he had gang land connections of some description."

"Erm, yes, I see what you mean, but no, I have no idea who he was linked to, I was just surmising."

"And, I'm afraid, I have to ask you this, but what about Linda?" Czerniak asked, as he leant forward over the desk, "did you ever suspect, that she might be linked in some way to an organised crime group?"

"What, was she involved in drugs or, some gangster's moll?" He replied angrily, "no, she wasn't and, before that bastard Sunderland turned her head, she was just an ordinary housewife, my wife."

"And finally," Czerniak said quietly, "can you think of anyone, who would want to do her any harm?"

"No, no one," he replied, sobbing once again, "yes, we'd had our ups and downs, I think most couples do but, until that bastard, inveigled his way into our lives, we were, or, I thought we were happy."

Chapter 5.

"So, how did you two get on at the scene?" Czerniak asked Danny Murphy and Tony Smith after he'd finished briefing them on the interview with Superintendent Griffiths.

"This whole bloody job is bloody odd from start to finish," Tony Smith replied, "I mean, did you know, that immediately after the forensics team finished dusting the scene, the place was sealed up and no buggers been inside since?"

"Hmm, that doesn't surprise me, in the least," Czerniak said, in disgust, "because, from what I can gather so far, the Chief Super in charge of professional standards, having heard we were being called in, saw his arse and, put an immediate stop, to any form of enquires being carried out."

"Oh, well, that will explain why our DI Jones, was so bloody sheepish, when I asked him about the house to house enquiries."

"Yes, and yet again, I'm not surprised because, no bugger has done any," Czerniak said angrily, "anyway, what do you make of the Superintendent's account?"

"Well, having been to the scene and, now knowing the layout and where the bodies were found, I'd have to say, that to me, it doesn't quite make sense," DS Tony Smith said, as he made himself a cup of tea, "because, according to the preliminary forensic report, which the DI gave us, Sunderland had been shot in the head and therefore, one would presume, he died almost instantly, whereas, our female victim, having been shot three times in the body, would have bled out far slower, so, if, as the Superintendent says, after he tried to revive her, did he go on, to deliberately contaminated the other body with his DNA."

"I agree, but there again, he did say, that ambulance control asked if Sunderland was dead and, if as he says, he was in shock, maybe he fumbled around the guys neck and, just thought he felt a pulse," Czerniak replied, still deep in thought, "I mean, put yourself in his position, you know, you've just found your wife, dead, in a pool of blood."

"Yeh, I get all that boss, but I still think it's all a bit too convenient though, don't you?" Tony asked, "I mean, by transferring his DNA, onto both bodies, in some vain attempt at resuscitating two people who were already dead, he would have known, it was going to take him out of the picture, forensic wise, straight away."

"Yes, I agree and, if that is the case then, not only is he a cold and calculating murderer, he's also very devious and, even though I don't think he's told us everything, I still get the distinct feeling, that he's neither of those."

"What did Rajni think of him?" Danny asked.

"Erm, to be honest with you, I don't actually know, because as we came out of the interview room, she had a phone call and, had to dash back to the hotel for something."

With a map of the streets, around Bryn Forydd Road and, some still photographs, taken by the forensic team, the two detectives then, talked Czerniak through the murder scene.

With its neatly manicured front lawn, thirty-two, Bryn Forydd Road, was one of many, reasonably smart, recently built, detached houses, on a small estate, situated, just west of Rhyl town centre.

On the face of it, there were no physical signs of a forced entry into the property and, although the metal plate around the front door lock, was heavy scratched, it was unbroken and therefore, it was assumed, that the offenders, had either let themselves in with a key or, had been invited inside, by one, or both of the victims.

The woodblock flooring in the hallway, where Superintendent Griffiths, had attempted to resuscitate Garry Sunderland, still bore bloodstains as did, a Persian style rug in the kitchen, where Mrs Griffiths' body had been found.

Having examined every room in the house, for signs of a struggle, the Forensic scientists believed, that someone, wearing gloves, had searched several drawers and, a walk-in wardrobe however, without the awaited SOCO report, this fact could neither be confirmed or denied.

Outside, there were two cars parked on the driveway, the red Mazda MX5, owned by Mrs Griffiths and, a dark grey Mercedes B class, which was registered to Sunderland Motors, Coast Road, Kinmel Bay, Rhyl.

Both cars were locked however, when the Mercedes was examined, a forensics officer, found a holdall, containing men's clothing, a one-way plane ticket to Istanbul and, a passport in the name of Georgio Cartulary but, bearing Garry Sunderland's photograph.

"Have we any idea, who this Cartulary character is," Czerniak asked, "or why he's using Sunderland's photograph?"

"None and, as that Chief Super pulled the plug on any local investigations, more or less, before it could even be started, nobody has made any attempt to find out yet," Tony Smith replied.

"Well, that's your first priority and secondly, see if you can chase up the SOCCO report, in the meantime, now that our wandering colleague has returned," Czerniak said, after seeing Rajni walk through the door, "we can head over to Kinmel Bay and search Sunderland's showroom, which I'm afraid Danny, leaves you, to start those, bloody house to house enquiries."

"Huh, cheers boss," Danny replied, as he picked up his briefcase.

"Did you get whatever it was you needed," Czerniak asked, as he and Rajni headed for the car.

"What, oh yeh, silly really, as I found it in the bottom of my handbag," she replied, without indicating what she was talking about.

The conversation, on their fifteen-minute journey to Kinmel Bay, was mainly about the interview with Superintendent Griffiths, with Rajni, mostly agreeing with Czerniak's view of the man.

Set on a large corner plot, just off the main coast road, in Kinmel Bay, the showrooms of Sunderland Motors, with its large name plate, painted in black and gold, looked quite impressive, as did the forecourt, which boasted several Mercedes, BMWs and, an immaculate, old Jaguar XJ10.

"Bloody hell, there's some money's worth sitting out here," Rajni remarked, as they pulled up on the forecourt.

"Yeh, but have you seen what's inside," Czerniak said, pointing towards the showroom window and, the two Maserati sports cars on display.

Having donned, white forensic suits, gloves and overshoes, they unlocked the front door however, as they entered the showroom, both of them, were immediately struck, by the strong smell of bleach.

"Some bugger has beaten us to it," Czerniak growled, as he pushed open an office door, to see, that the desk and filling cabinet drawers were all open.

"Same in there," Rajni said, as she came out of a store room, "plus, there's a small window, that looks like it's been forced open."

"Big enough for someone to get through?"

"Yeh, providing they weren't too fat," she replied with a smile.

"Question is, was it broken into, before or after the killings?" Czerniak remarked, as he scanned the office, looking for some form of CCTV device.

"There's no way of telling," Rajni replied, whilst looking at a list of cars, the showroom had for sale, "but, I think, there's a Mercedes A class missing."

"Are you sure?" Czerniak asked, as he tried following a length of black cable, hoping it would lead to a CCTV recorder.

"Well, according to his diary, it looks like he took one in, as a part ex, two weeks prior to the killings and, I've just checked this bunch of key fobs against the list and, it's the only one missing," she replied, whilst double checking the sales ledger, "plus, there's nothing here to show it's been sold."

"Odd car to steal though, especially when you've got all those high-powered jobs outside. What was it, a special edition thing or something?" Czerniak asked, as he found the cut end of the CCTV cable, "shit, well that explains why we can't find a recording device, as some buggers cut the wire and nicked it."

"I'll get on blower to D/I Jones," Rajni said, pulling out her mobile phone, as she moved slowly, into a large walk-in cupboard, "and ask him to get someone to trawl through the CCTV for the night of the killings."

"Good idea," Czerniak shouted, as he squeezed behind a cabinet, in his quest to find another CCTV recording device.

"Someone's had a go at this safe too," Rajni called out, from the walk-in cupboard at the back of the office.

"Hmm, looks like chisel marks," Czerniak remarked, as he joined Rajni in the cupboard, "best get a SOCO team in here and a locksmith, so we can have a look inside and see what they were after."

As they sat outside in the car, waiting for the scenes of crime officers to arrive, Czerniak contacted D/I Jones.

"Hello Mel, it's us again," Czerniak said, when the D/I answered his phone, "what's your feelings about this break in at Sunderland's car showroom."

"Do you think it's connected to the murders?"

"Yes, I think so, but I'd value your opinion, you know, as the local man, so to speak."

"Well, the simple answer is, that I couldn't say one way or the other, because just lately, Kinmel Bay has been blighted, by a series of similar burglaries."

"Shit, is anyone in the frame for them?"

"Huh, you can take your pick from about ten or so local villains," he replied, with a slight chuckle, "but I'm afraid, our greatest problem comes from further afield."

"Liverpool?"

"Yes, there and Manchester, because we have groups of young lads, coming here on holiday and, as a parting gift, they either break into a neighbouring caravan or, one of the local business premises."

"When you say, groups, how many are we talking about?"

"Well, let me put it into some sort of context for you, at the height of the summer, we have a weekly, transient population, of about a hundred thousand and, whereas a high proportion of those, are law abiding families, there is also a certain element, who will have stolen a car to get here and no doubt, will steal one for their return journey."

"And, is that what you think has happened here?"

"It's a strong possibility and, with the Easter bank holiday just behind us, most of the twenty or so caravan camps, dotted along the coast here, will still bel quite full."

The fact, that the local area had been plagued by burglaries over the Easter bank holiday, was later confirmed by Brian Thompson, the scenes of crime officer, after he finished examining the scene for fingerprints.

"I'm afraid, it's got all the hallmarks, of three other breaks I've been to in this last week alone," he said with a weary smile, as he took, his white forensic suit off, "entry through a tiny window, neat search of drawers etc and, something you don't often see, nicking the CCTV player."

"So, that's happened on a previous occasion?"

"Yes, last Thursday, at the newsagent's shop, about a hundred yards or so, further down the Coast Road," he replied, whilst pointing in that general direction, "and the Ship Launch, the previous weekend."

"And how did they get in?"

"Erm, the newsagent's, was similar to this one, entry through a small window but, with regards to the pub, we think the offenders may have been hiding in the toilets, as there were no tool marks on the window, they used as an exit point."

"And, what about cars, were any stolen during, or after those other break ins?" Czerniak asked, as Brian Thompson began loading his equipment into the rear of the white van.

"Not from any of the attacked the premises no," he replied, whilst wiping his hands on a towel, "sorry, but I hate the powder in these gloves. Sorry, yes, you were asking about cars, no, like I said, none from the actual addresses but, a Ford Kuga was taken off of a driveway on the same night the pub was broken into."

"How far from the premises?"

"Oh, good question, erm, let me see, fifty to sixty yards, yeh, no further than that and, if I'm not mistaken, it was found abandoned not far from the Runcorn Bridge."

"Where?"

"Oh yeh, sorry, yes, erm, on the outskirts of Liverpool."

Chapter 6.

Having gained nothing, other than, some rather conflicting theories regarding the burglary in the car showroom, they returned to St Asaph and, their mini incident room.

"Any luck with that passport," Czerniak asked Tony Smith, as he poured himself a cup of coffee.

"Well, according to the Home Office, the passport is genuine enough but, who the hell Georgio Cartulary is, or was, I have no idea."

"Was the plane ticket, in the same name as the passport?"

"It was, but paid for, with Sunderland's credit card."

"So, the question is, if it was Sunderland who paid for the ticket, why was he flying to Istanbul last Sunday under a false name and, not under his own."

"Maybe the answer is in his safe," Rajni said, as she put the phone down, "seems the locksmith has managed to open it and apparently, its stuffed full of documents."

"Good, can you nip back there and pick them up, as I need to find D/I Jones."

With Tony Smith continuing his internet search for the mysterious Georgio Cartulary and Rajni, heading back to Kinmel Bay, Czerniak went downstairs to find D/I Mel Jones.

However, as he approached the Detective Inspectors', glass fronted office, he was surprised to see Superintendent Griffiths sitting alone at the desk.

"Erm, hello sir," Czerniak said politely as he entered through the open door, "I thought, with you saying you wanted to avoid everyone, you would be on compassionate leave."

"What, no, I mean, what would be the point in sitting alone in that big house, when I can be of some use here," he said, looking and sounding slightly distracted, "no, I'll just have grin and bare it, anyway, were you after Mel."

"Erm, yes sir, is he around."

"In the general office I think, said he was going to brief the lads, who are working overtime tonight."

"Big job?"

"What, oh, no, there's been a spate of breaks on the patch, so he's putting together a team to keep obs on some likely, target premises."

"Tell me sir, does the name Georgio Cartulary mean anything to you?"

"No, not off the top of my head, why, who is he?"

"Oh, it's just a line of enquiry we're following, look sir, if you're still here when the D/I returns, can you ask him to give me a call please," Czerniak said as he left the office.

"This job gets stranger by the minute," Tony Smith muttered, more to himself than anyone else, "as, according to Google, this Cartulary character is, Inter Milan's goalie."

"Is there a picture of him," Czerniak asked as he walked over to the laptop computer, Tony Smith was using.

"Yeh and, as you can see, looks nothing like our man."

"Is it a coincidence or what?"

"I couldn't tell you boss, but he's the only Cartulary I could find on the internet."

Half an hour later, their hopes of getting some answers, suddenly grew, a hundred-fold, when Rajni returned, with a bundle of documents, some of which, related to someone called, Georgio Cartulary.

"What is he, some sort of money lender," Tony Smith asked, as he joined the other two, to help sift through the documents.

"Yeh, but I'm beginning to think he and Sunderland are the same person which, would certainly explain, how he was financing his car business, because those two Maserati sports jobs, must have cost a small fortune," Czerniak replied.

"Of course," Rajni suddenly blurted out, after she'd found a ledger, detailing addresses in various middle eastern countries, "he's been running, an Hawala Banking system."

"A what system?" Czerniak asked, totally confused and taken aback, by her sudden outburst.

"An Hawala Banking system," she replied, amazed, that neither man knew what she was talking about, "you know, a money transfer business, where you go into a shop, say in London, hand over five hundred pounds and, after a few phone calls, your relative in Delhi goes into his local Hawala bank and picks up the equivalent in Rupees."

"Yeh, yeh, I think I've heard of them," Czerniak said, still not fully understanding what she meant.

"The only question is, what is a small-time car dealer, based in rural Wales, doing, running a money transfer business, as surely, there can't be a call for it out here in the sticks," she said, now beginning to question the theory herself."

"Well I don't see it myself," Tony said, scratching his head, "I mean, it's just as easy, to do a bloody, electronic bank transfer isn't it?"

"Well, for one thing, there is little or no outside control, over any of the transactions," Rajni replied, now more certain of her theory, "meaning its very popular with certain communities and of course, people who want to launder their money."

"Well, if he was running some sort of money laundering scheme, it might explain, why Sunderland was using an alias and possibly, give us a motive for the killings."

"Christ, have you seen the sums involved," Tony said, as he thumbed through a small ledger, "we're talking serious money here and I mean serious."

"Enough to kill him for?" Czerniak asked.

"Well, in this one transaction alone," Tony replied, pointing to an entry in the ledger, "he transferred fifty thousand, to someone in Morocco."

"Any names or addresses of these clients?" Czerniak asked, as he peered at the ledger, over Tony's shoulder, "because the sooner we find out who they are, the sooner we can eliminate them from the enquiry."

"No, as you can see, it's all in some kind of number code," he replied, showing the page to Czerniak.

"What about the recipients, can we at least identify any of them?"

"No, all we've got, is the address of the bank the money was sent to and from and then, it's just that same series of numbers."

"I think, that's how it works," Rajni said, deep in thought and, ignoring the conversation about money laundering, "because, a few years ago, I remember my father sent some money to his brother in India and, all he had to do, was supply details of which town the money was going to and, a code word, known only to his brother."

"And the money, how is that sent?" Czerniak asked, curious to learn everything he could about the system.

"Erm, yes, it's difficult to explain because, from what I recall, it was all done on trust and, as far as I know, no money is actually, you know, physically transferred between the two banks at the time."

"Well how does that work then?" Tony asked, his face displaying the total confusion he felt, "because to me, it doesn't make much sense, I mean, if your father took money into his local bank thing."

"Hawala," Rajni added.

"Yeh, whatever it's called," Tony said, still looking confused, "so, say he took, five hundred quid into that bank in London, are you saying, that it stayed there and, was never actually sent to India?"

"Yes, I think so, look, don't quote me on this, because it was a few years ago and, well, I didn't take that much interest at the time,"

Rajni replied, as she tried to find a way of explaining how the system worked, "but from what I can remember, is that it's all done on mutual trust between banks."

"What, like I'll pay you the money, but not today?" Tony Smith said with a laugh, still convinced that Sunderland had been running some sort of money laundering scam.

"No, not quite like that," she replied, now getting slightly frustrated with the fact, that Tony was not, or refusing to understanding what she was trying to say, "so, this is, how I think it works and, very much like the modern bank transfer, the sending bank, keeps the deposited money and, the receiving one, say in Delhi, pays out in local currency and then, when money is sent in the opposite direction, the Rupees are kept in India and the bank in this country, pays out in pounds sterling, like I said, it's all done, very much on trust."

"But surely, there must be some sort of system, where these two banks level up what's owed, because I should imagine, in the main, its one-way traffic," Czerniak said, still not convinced he understood the system either.

"Well, unlike modern, main stream banks, who I think transport vast amounts between each other, I think they have traditionally used a courier, you know, to transport the money between countries."

"That might explain, why Sunderland was supposed to be flying to Istanbul last Sunday," Tony said, "you know, carrying a load of cash."

"Yeh, that just might be the answer," Czerniak replied, "and, if that was the case, then the proof may well be in these documents, so grab a handful each and get reading."

For more than an hour, the only sounds that could be heard in the incident room, were the occasion clink of a coffee cup or a spoon, being discarded, back into the sugar bowl.

"According to this," Tony said quietly, whilst still looking down at a page in one of the ledgers, "the equivalent of twenty thousand pounds, is being transferred to Istanbul, on the fourteenth of every month."

"Don't suppose there's any details of the clients?" Czerniak asked.

"No, just these bloody number codes," he replied, "but the thing is, it was the fourteenth last Friday, so, what if, this isn't a domestic murder after all."

"Good point Tony," Czerniak said, now deep in thought, "and, it was either a robbery gone wrong or, it was a disgruntled customer who thought Sunderland was ripping them off."

"Might explain, why he was shot in the head, almost execution style and she wasn't," Tony added.

"Which would point more to money laundering," Rajni said, thinking her theory of a Hawala bank was slowly disappearing.

"Yeh, well, let's not jump to any conclusions and instead, concentrate on finding Sunderland's code system because, I think it holds the answer."

"Just a thought boss," Rajni said, some half an hour later, "but could these code numbers, be part of his clients phone number."

"Jesus, what a good shout, where's his bloody mobile phone," Czerniak demanded with some urgency.

Within twenty minutes of opening the phone, they had a list of at least fifteen potential customers, who'd either been using

Sunderland to launder money or, if Rajni was right, to transfer money abroad.

They also had the name Ahmet Yilmaz, which they linked to the code, 30069181, the number being used, in connection with those, twenty thousand-pound, monthly payments to, a so-called Hawala bank, in Istanbul.

As Tony scanned the social media and then, the on-line telephone directory, Rajni contacted the PNC operator and ran a check on Ahmet Yilmaz.

"Nothing on PNC," Rajni declared as she put the phone down.

"Same on Facebook and Google," Tony added, "but, he might be the guy running the Last Ottoman Kebab and Grill, in somewhere called, Colwyn Bay because, there's a Mr A. Yilmaz listed as the owner."

"Colwyn Bay, is about fifteen miles down the coast from here," Czerniak said, with a broad grin, "so not too far away, well done you lot, come on, time to pack it in for the night."

"What about Danny?" Rajni asked, concerned for her colleague's welfare.

"Christ, good point," Czerniak replied, as he picked up his mobile phone.

"Hi boss," the weary voice, on the other end of the phone said.

"Any joy?"

"Huh, seems the average age of people living in that road is twenty-five and, as most of them were out on the town last Friday night, none of them saw or heard anything."

"What, not even a raised voice?" Czerniak asked, surprised at the poor results, from the house to house enquiries in Bryn Forydd Road.

"Well, that's just it, because it's normal, for so many of them to be out and about on a Friday night, you know, with car doors slamming and neighbours laughing and joking loudly, no one took any notice or, more to the point, heard anything out of the ordinary."

"What about unusual vehicles, or people hanging around?"

"Again, I drew a blank and, because many of them used various taxis."

"No one took notice of any strange cars," Czerniak said, cutting across Danny.

"You've got it in one boss," he replied.

"What about Sunderland, did anyone have anything to say about him?"

"Erm, well, there was quite an interesting comment from the Sanderson's, the people living at number twenty-seven, which is just opposite the scene," Danny replied, "which is, they were surprised to see Mrs Griffiths living with Sunderland, as they thought he was gay."

"Gay, where the hell, did they get that idea from, as according to John Griffiths, half the married men in Rhyl were after Sunderland because, he'd been trying to seduce their wives."

"Well, it was more Mrs Sanderson than her husband," Danny replied with a slight chuckle, "maybe Sunderland rejected her or something, but she couldn't understand why, and I quote, 'such a glamorous woman, would move in with him, especially, as he only ever seems to entertain men' un quote."

"Aye, like you say, there's nothing like a woman scorned," Czerniak said, joining in, the light-hearted banter, "so, apart from that little gem, nothing of any value?"

"No, sorry."

"Well, at least you tried, which is more than can be said for the locals, anyway, were calling it a day, so, we'll see you back at the hotel."

Chapter 7.

As they headed back to the hotel that night, Rajni seemed unusually quiet and, concerned there might be a problem, Czerniak asked if she was okay.

"What, oh yeh, just thinking things over that's all," she replied, whilst staring out of the passenger window.

"Are you sure, because sometimes, especially when you're away from home, small problems can seem so much bigger."

"No, it's nothing, I'm fine, honest."

"Is it something to do with you having to dash back to the hotel this morning?" He persisted.

"Look boss, it's nothing okay," she replied sharply, "I'm sorry, I didn't mean to snap, but I just need some head space, you know, to work things out in my mind."

"Okay, point taken, but if there is anything, my door is always open."

"Thanks, boss, I appreciate that."

With remainder of the journey, travelled in total silence, Czerniak was somewhat relieved when they finally pulled into the hotel carpark.

As Tony and Danny ate their evening meal, they speculated at length, as to why, Mrs Sanderson thought Gary Sunderland was gay.

Then, once they'd exhausted that subject, their conversation turned to Mr Yilmaz and, why they thought, he was sending so much money to Turkey each month.

Whilst contributing the odd comment to the discussion, Czerniak's attention, was mainly on Rajni, who throughout the meal, had merely pushed her food, aimlessly around the plate and, not eaten a thing.

"Well I reckon it's drugs, what do you think boss?" Tony asked and then, when he saw Czerniak was distracted, he repeated the question, "what do you reckon boss?"

"What, oh yeh, drugs every time," he replied, still not fully concentrating on the conversation, "look, if it's okay with you three, I'm going to have an early night as I'm absolutely knackered."

"Yeh, I won't be far behind, it's been a long day," Rajni added.

"Now don't stay up too long you two, not on a school night," Czerniak said with a broad grin, before heading towards the staircase.

"Okay dad," Tony replied.

"Big hat," Czerniak called out, then, just as he disappeared upstairs, "a big black one, with a shiny badge on the front."

Having poured himself a generous glass of whisky, Czerniak went through into the en-suite and turned on the shower.

Then, just as he was unbuttoning his shirt, he heard a gentle tap on his room door and, thinking it might be a member of the hotel staff, he partially opened it and peered out into the corridor.

"Bloody hell Rajni, I thought it was room service," he said, whilst hurriedly buttoning up his shirt, "what's up?"

"Can I come in?" She asked, with a certain amount of urgency in her voice.

"Erm, well, it's a bit late and erm," he started to say, before she pushed past him and entered the room.

"Er, well come in why don't you," he said, whilst checking down the corridor in both directions.

"Can I have one of those?" She asked, pointing to his whisky.

"Erm, yeh, but I thought you didn't drink, I mean, isn't it against your religion or something?"

"My family are Hindu not Muslims," she snapped, before immediately apologising, "look, I'm sorry right, it's just, well, because I'm a little darker than the rest of you, people automatically assume that I'm some sort of terrorist."

"No, it's me that's sorry Rajni, I had no idea," he said, handing her, the glass of whisky he'd poured for himself, "I mean, call me ignorant if you must, but I know you're Hindu and, well I just thought it was one of those things you didn't do, because, whenever we've gone to the pub, you always have a soft drink."

"Do I?"

"Well, erm, well on the few occasions I've been out with you lot, you have."

"Sorry, sorry, sorry, it's just me being sensitive," she said taking a large sip of the whisky, "ooh, that's rather smooth."

"Yes, it's called West Cork," he told her whilst pouring himself a glass, "apparently, after its been triple distilled, its stored for several months in wooden, bourbon casks."

"Really interesting," she said, looking totally uninterested in the facts he was quoting from the bottles label.

"Sorry, yes, bit of a whisky nerd," he said, having realised, that she wasn't in the slightest bit interested, "so, what's all this about, because you've been acting strange most of the day."

"Erm, have I, yes, I'm sorry about that boss," she replied, before sitting in the only armchair in the room.

"For Christ sake Rajni, stop saying you're sorry," he said, rather sharper than he intended, before mellowing his voice to say, "and, stop calling me boss, when we're off duty, my name's bloody Jack."

"Sorry boss, I mean erm Jack," she said nervously, before having another glug of whisky, "but things have got a bit out of hand today and, and erm, well, I need to tell someone or, my head is going to explode."

"Well, look, you sit there and let me turn my shower off," he said, nodding towards the en-suite.

Then, on his return, he topped up both glasses with ice and whisky before sitting on the end of his bed.

"So, what's wrong, and, don't try fobbing me off by saying you're fine, because your obviously not."

"Erm, well, look, before I tell you anything, you have to promise not to get angry," she said, before taking a large glug of whisky.

"Yes, I promise, now get a move on before my ice melts."

"Hmm, very funny," she said with a nervous grin, "but seriously, I only did it, well, because I'd heard you lying to Andrews."

"Lying, about what?"

"About those files you've taken from the archives."

"Files, what files?" Czerniak said, now getting to his feet to pace around.

"Those bloody sudden death files, you left out on display on this coffee table," she replied, whilst pointing towards the now bare table top, "the ones I saw, when I came in to collect your briefcase earlier."

"Shit, I gave you my keys, didn't I?"

"Yeh, well, if you remember, you were busy talking to the DCI at the time and, if I'm not mistaken, telling him, you hadn't taken any files and then."

"You came in here and saw them."

"And, call me a nosey cow if you like," she started to say, before he interrupted.

"You read them."

"Well, only to scan them briefly and, I must admit for a time, couldn't work out why you wanted them," she replied, "but then, on the way over to St Asaph, you said something about the Glendenning case."

"And put two and two together?"

"Well, not at first no, which is why I made an excuse to come back here."

"To read them?"

"Yes, but I was still a little confused, because I thought the case was shut, which is why, I phoned a friend in the file preparation unit."

"And they told you, that Glendenning's brief, was asking for a judicial review of the case, because I'd tricked his client, into making a false confession, which he now wishes to retract."

"Something along those lines yes."

"So, why are you so worried, I mean, it's going to be common knowledge any day now."

"Well, I thought, you know, with you digging around in those old files, that you were trying to find additional evidence, to strengthen the case against Glendenning."

"And, you thought right."

"Which is why, I telephoned Hannah, you know, Hannah Hightown, the woman Glendenning had a brief fling with."

"Yes, I know who you mean," Czerniak replied, whilst trying to contain his temper, "but why would you contact her, as she's already told us everything she knows, hasn't she?"

"Well, to a point yes," Rajni said, before taking another large gulp of whisky, "you see, when I first spoke with her, she told me quite a few things about Glendenning which, because they weren't exactly relevant to case, weren't included in her original statement, like for instance, how, before she divorced him, his wife was running her own successful business, but nevertheless, he still tried to control every aspect of her life."

"Yes, when we interviewed him, I got the impression, that he was some sort of control freak, but what has that, got to do with the case."

"Well, it seems the company she runs, over in Pimlico, is called Photofix and, among the many processes they carry out, is one, where they apparently, transform 35 mil film and old still photographs into a digital format, which is then downloaded into a perpetually picture frame, whatever that means," she said waving a hand in the air.

"Yeh, I think I know what you mean, but I still don't see where you're going with this."

"Well, according to our Hannah," she replied, before taking another sip of her whisky, "whilst they were having a lunchtime session, in some hotel room, Glendenning took a phone call from his wife, who by all accounts was none too happy."

"No, I bet she wasn't."

"Christ, I wish you'd concentrate on the story and stop making up your own endings," she said before continuing, "anyway, it seems, his wife told him over the phone, that she'd just caught a member of staff stealing or thought she had."

"And?" Czerniak asked impatiently.

"And, when she confronted the young girl concerned, she in turn, claimed it was Glendenning who was the thief."

"Glendenning, how, why?"

"Well, according to the girl, who Mrs Glendenning was about to sack, she'd seen him in there on more than one occasion, using the Photofix account, to place orders for goods and then, when the delivery driver arrived with the orders, our doctor, was always conveniently on hand, to take delivery."

"And what, took whatever it was away with him?"

"Exactly."

"And what did he have to say about it?"

"Huh, categorically denied any involvement to his wife but then, when he got off the phone, he apparently laughed out loud and called her a stupid bitch."

"I take it, you're talking about his wife?"

"Yes, and, to rub salt into the wounds, as he got back into bed, he bragged about how he'd been using her company account for weeks, to obtain products for use in his clinical trials."

"What sort of products?"

"Well, I have to warn you, because I think, this where, you're going to get angry with me," she replied, before draining her glass.

"Christ, go on, what have you done?"

"I erm, well, and, only because I had to know what it was he'd been ordering," she replied nervously, "I, erm, I telephoned Mrs Glendenning and, erm, pretended to be a lawyer, involved in an unfair dismissal case."

"You did what?" he practically yelled.

"I pretended to be a lawyer," she replied quietly, "and, that I was erm, erm working on an industrial tribunal case involving her former employee and, that she was duty bound to tell me about the circumstances, which led to her sacking that member of staff."

"Jesus Christ, no wonder you thought I'd lose it," Czerniak said, though this time somewhat quieter.

"Yes, well, look, I obviously didn't give my name but, perhaps when you hear what she had to say, you might not be so angry."

"Bloody hell, get on with it," he said, his anger still visible in his voice, whilst pouring himself another whisky.

"Erm, well, from what she said, this girl had placed several orders, for goods they no longer used in their chemical processes and, when confronted had lied about her involvement. But then, when I pushed Mrs Glendenning further, she said that the girl had come up with some absurd suggestion, that it was her ex-husband, who, had not only placed the order, but had taken the goods directly from the delivery driver," she replied, whilst holding out her empty glass.

"So, we have this young girl, making unsubstantiated claims, that he's a thief, how does that strengthen our case against Glendenning."

"Ah yes, but the goods, we're talking about, weren't as you might imagine, very valuable or, contained in some huge packing case, or parcel, they were, in fact, inside, quite a small and securely sealed metal box," she said, raising her now full glass in salute, "containing a powder, called Potassium Cyanide."

"What?" He practically yelled.

"Potassium Cyanide," she repeated, "which I believe, is the same substance, which we say, he used to kill all of his victims."

"Jesus Christ, Jesus bloody Christ," Czerniak said quietly, "did she give you the name of the suppliers."

"No, in fact, when I asked for those details, you know, so I could verify, if my client had placed the order or not, she was most vague."

"Vague?" Czerniak asked.

"Well, let's just say, she wasn't going to tell a total stranger over the telephone."

"So, did you get the feeling, that she didn't altogether trust her ex-husband?"

"I don't know about that, but she was definitely hiding something."

Chapter 8.

"But you still haven't told me, where this new information came from," DCI Andrews said over the phone, the following morning.

"Let's just say, it's a reliable source," Czerniak replied, with a broad grin, he knew Andrews couldn't see, "and, I think we need to act on it as soon as possible."

"And, when we confront Mrs Glendenning, are we to quote this source of yours?" he asked cautiously.

"Look boss, if I was you, all I would tell her, is, that a former member of staff has made certain allegations of theft against her ex-husband," Czerniak replied, hoping that Andrews wouldn't ask any more awkward questions.

"Yes, but is that true?"

"One hundred per cent because, for one thing, those very same allegations, were made directly to her, before she sacked the member of staff making them."

"A bit odd though isn't it, that a friend of this former member of staff, should contact you now and, just out of the blue?" Andrews said, still not convinced that Czerniak was telling him everything.

"No, not really, I mean, when you think, it was only last week, that Glendenning was granted bail and, with it being reported in all the papers, you know, about the cyanide, well, it must have somehow jolted something in her memory, which in turn, prompted her to come forward," Czerniak replied quickly.

"But how did she get your number?"

"Erm, switchboard apparently," Czerniak replied, still hoping that his boss would just accept what he was saying and stop asking awkward questions.

"Did Mrs Glendenning's company ever use cyanide?"

"Erm, I'm not too sure on that one, but, if you recall, back in the early part of the investigation, we were looking for companies, who used cyanide to developed film, which is, one of the processes Photofix, apparently, carries out," he replied, hoping that final fact would be enough to convince Andrews.

"Right, leave it with me, I'll get someone over to get a detailed statement from her today," Andrews said, before asking Czerniak, how his current case was going.

With DCI Andrews updated on events in North Wales and happy, in his own mind anyway, that progress was taking place on the Glendenning case, Czerniak went downstairs for breakfast.

Then, twenty minutes later, whilst Tony and Danny, headed to St Asaph, to dig deeper into the Hawala bank ledgers and then, search for a real bank account, where all the money was hopefully being held, Czerniak and Rajni travelled down the coast to Colwyn Bay.

"What have you done, about, you know, erm, what I erm, told you last night," she asked awkwardly, once she and Czerniak were alone in the car.

"Passed it on to the DCI of course," he replied, in rather a formal manner.

"So, does that mean my days on C.I.D. are numbered?"

"Why?"

"Well, you know, because of the way I gained the information," she replied quietly.

"What information?" he questioned.

"About Glendenning, using his wife's company account to buy the cyanide," she replied, rather confused buy his evasive manner.

"Oh, the information, which came from a friend of the former employee, who incidentally, telephoned me, out of the blue last night," he replied, whilst continuing to look straight ahead and avoid her gaze.

"Bloody hell boss, you didn't tell him that?"

"Why not, it's the truth isn't it, I mean, you were in the car when I received the call, weren't you?" he replied, now turning to face her.

"What, oh yeh, absolutely," then after a brief pause, "bloody hell, thanks boss."

"For what?"

"For being, not only my boss, but a bloody good friend as well."

"Yes, well, don't make a habit of it, or you'll find yourself, lying in a shop doorway somewhere, covered in piss, alongside Johnny Lightbown," he replied with a slight chuckle.

"Christ, perish the thought," she said, with a horrified look on her face, "I mean, how the hell does he do it, day after day?"

"It's his thing though isn't it," Czerniak replied, before pausing to recall an event involving DC Johnny Lightbown, "Christ, yeh, I remember when we were both still young and, in many ways, still green, well I was anyway, and we were seconded onto the drugs squad, to watch a dealer, who was thought to be stashing gear in Epping Forest."

"Bloody hell boss, Epping Forest, it's bloody huge isn't it," she said, interrupting his story.

"Exactly, which is why, Johnny, me and four other, naïve young bobbies were, basically dumped there and told to spread out and find a hiding place," he replied, "well, whilst I and the others looked for a bush or a tree to hide behind, Johnny dug a hole and buried himself."

"He did what?"

"Apparently, he'd brought one of those collapsible spade things with him and, used it to dig a hole and then, he, sort of buried the best part of his body, before sticking a clump of dead ferns on his head."

"Crikey, what was he, ex SAS or something?" She asked, with a slight chuckle.

"No, honestly, like I say, it was his thing and, because Johnny was the one who clocked the dealer digging up his stash of heroin, the drug squad held on to him."

"So, how long has he been there?"

"Best part of twenty years, maybe longer."

"Christ, can you imagine being married to someone like that and, him coming home stinking of piss every night."

"Hmm, which is probably why, none of his marriages worked out."

"But credit where credit is due boss, that's some dedication to the job."

"Yeh, what you might call, going, over and beyond, but knowing him as I do, I don't think he would have wanted it any other way."

Using the cars satnav system, they easily located Greenfield Road and, half way along its tree lined pavement, The Last Ottoman, Kebab and Grill restaurant.

As they entered the establishment, a young, dark haired man, of Mediterranean appearance, rushed forward to politely inform them, that the restaurant didn't open for business until midday.

"That's okay son," Czerniak said, in a friendly and calm manner, "we're from the police and, we'd like to have a few words with your boss, is he around?"

"Erm, I'm afraid Mr Yilmaz isn't here yet," he replied nervously, after hearing they were police officers, "has, erm, something happened."

"What time are you expecting him?" Czerniak asked, ignoring the young man's question.

"He, erm, he normally arrives about eleven thirty."

"Hmm, it's only nine fifteen, is there any chance you could phone him and ask him to come in sooner," Czerniak asked, again trying to sound calm and relaxed.

"Erm, er yes, can I tell him what it's about," the young man said, as he pulled a mobile phone from his pocket.

"Well, here's the thing," Czerniak said, looking him directly in the face, "it is, something of a delicate and private matter and one, I don't think I should discuss, without his express permission."

Having gulped audibly, the young man rushed out of the dining area and, through a set of swing doors, only to return, five minutes later, with a tray, containing two cups of coffee, a milk jug and some wrapped sugar cubes.

"Erm, Mr Yilmaz will be with you in about twenty minutes," he said, as he placed the tray on a table, "in the meantime, he suggests you enjoy a coffee."

Dressed in a dark suit, with a crisp, white open necked shirt and, recently coiffured hair, Ahmet Yilmaz, was a smart looking man, in his mid-fifties.

"I must apologize for my son," he said, after shaking their hands, "he should have offered you a glass of water with your coffee."

"No, it's fine, we both like our coffee strong," Czerniak replied with a smile, "please, will you join us, as we would like to ask you a few questions."

"Yes of course," he said pulling out a seat, "so, tell me inspector, I'm intrigued to hear about this delicate matter you told my son about."

"I think you'll find, we only suggested we had a delicate matter to discuss," Czerniak replied with a polite smile, as he realised, it was the first time, that a member of the public had addressed him, as inspector, "so, can you tell me, how well you know a man, called Garry Sunderland?"

"I am sorry Inspector but, as far as I am aware, I have never met anyone of that name."

"What about, Georgio Cartulary?"

"Ah yes, him I know."

"How?"

"Well, it is, to use your phrase, a delicate matter," he replied, without answering the question.

"Yes, I appreciate that Mr Yilmaz, but I still need you to tell me, how you know him."

"We erm, we have occasionally done business together."

"What sort of business?"

"Well, he has handled one or two business transactions for me," he replied, still avoiding giving a direct answer.

"Monetary transactions?" Czerniak asked.

"Erm, yes, well, in a way, yes, one could say that."

"Bloody hell, it's like pulling teeth," Czerniak said, his patience disappearing fast, "look, we know he has been transferring money to Istanbul for you, once a month, so, the question I need answering, without any more of your bullshit, is why."

"Erm, yes, it is true, Mr Cartulary runs a Hawala bank and, helps me transfer money to my brother every month."

"For what reason?"

"Reason, you mean, why do I use Hawala bank and not British Bank?" he asked.

"Yes, well that and, why are you sending the money in the first place."

"Erm, it is difficult to explain."

"Is it because, Hawala have no connection to the British or Turkish government?" Rajni asked, leaning forward over the table, "which means, no one knows officially, just how much money you transfer."

"That is a slanderous thing to say, I am a British citizen and pay my taxes," he replied angrily.

"But not on the twenty grand, you send abroad every month," Czerniak said bluntly, "so, perhaps you'll answer the question, why are you sending money to Turkey every month?"

"My mother, she is sick with the cancer and my brother, he cannot afford the hospital bills, so I scrape together what I can each month and send it by Hawala."

"For how long?"

"Erm, only about eight months."

"And your mother, how is she?"

"Dying I'm afraid," he replied, his head nodding slightly, "mostly because, I have no more money to send."

"So, the twenty-thousand-pound money transfer, you made on the fourteenth of April, was that your most recent transaction with Mr Cartulary?"

"Yes, and very possibly my last, because, if I don't find a buyer for my house soon, I will have nothing left to send."

"And when, did you actually pay that money to Mr Cartulary?"

"Erm, it was on the Tuesday, the erm eleventh of this month."

"How well, did you know Mr Cartulary?"

"Erm, we were introduced at the mosque," he replied, "but apart from him arranging the money transfers, I have other no contact with him, why do you ask, has something happened to him?"

"I'm afraid, he was found dead, in the early hours of last Saturday morning," Czerniak replied, before looking Mr Yilmaz directly in the eyes to ask, "so, can you tell me, where you were, between, 10pm last Friday night and 2am Saturday morning."

"Erm, yes certainly, I would have been here," he said, with a certain amount of confidence, "because we had a birthday celebration booked and, I'm afraid to say, it went on until nearly 3am."

"And, just one more question, for now anyway, who else knew, how much money you were transferring every month?"

"Erm, besides my brother, no one."

"Not even your son?" Czerniak asked, whilst looking for some flicker of response in the face of Mr Yilmaz.

"What, Baris, no he knows nothing of this," he replied quickly, before the sudden realisation that Georgio Cartulary was dead, struck him, "you say, he died in the early hours of Saturday morning, can I ask how?"

"Well, we are treating his death as murder, if that helps you in any way," Czerniak said, as quietly as possible, as he felt Mr Yilmaz's son was listening in to their conversation.

"Murder, my god, my money, was it stolen?"

"I'm afraid I can't answer that question at this present time, except to say, that as yet, no large amounts of money have been found."

Chapter 9.

With the business address, of Yusuf Ozdemir, the man who had introduced, Mr Yilmaz to Georgio Cartulary, logged into their satnav, Czerniak and Rajni headed to the small seaside town of Penmaenmawr.

Once, a thriving community, thanks in the main, to the trade, created by a local granite quarry, the area fell into a spiral of decline when, without warning, it suddenly shut down production and then, only twelve months later, the A55 coast road, bypassed the town completely.

All along the road, leading into Penmaenmawr, the large Victorian and Edwardian buildings and houses, were testament to the former wealth of the town but, as most were now either flats or semi derelict, it also spoke quite loudly, of its rapid decline into abject poverty.

Just off Queens Street, in what would have once been, the main shopping area of the town and beneath, a black painted, but rather drab, wrought iron veranda, they found, the aptly named, Penmaenmawr Kebab House.

Obviously prewarned by his friend, Yusuf Ozdemir was waiting by the front door of his kebab house and, rather than let Czerniak and Rajni inside, he suggested they spoke in the police vehicle.

Wanting to see his face and, how he reacted to questioning, Czerniak told Mr Ozdemir to get into the back of the vehicle and then, climbed in beside him.

Then, with Mr Ozdemir giving directions, Rajni drove the car, to a remote parking area, on the rather down market and, noticeably deserted promenade.

"This place is dead," Rajni said out aloud, as she pulled into a parking space, "where is everyone."

"I'm afraid, this is as busy as it gets this time of the year," Yusuf replied.

"But Rhyl is heaving with holidaymakers," she countered.

"Yes, I know, I also have a shop there, but these days, I prefer the slower pace that this town offers, so I leave that part of the business, for my son to run."

"I take it, your friend has already told you what this about?" Czerniak asked.

"Yes, but I had no idea that Georgio was a Kafir," he replied.

"Sorry, he was a what?"

"A non-believer," he replied, "and, even though he was a Somali Italian or, said he was, he still prayed with us every Friday."

"At the mosque?"

"Yes, in Llandudno."

"Is that where you met him?"

"Yes, you see, although it is frowned on by many, the mosque is a good place to, how do you say it, network, is that the correct expression."

"If you mean, that you speak to other business people about business matters, then yes, networking is the correct expression."

"Which is how we met, I think, I was drinking tea with another friend, when Giorgio, if that's his real name, came over and started talking about the Hawala bank he was running in Kinmel Bay."

"Did you use it yourself?"

"Erm, to be honest, I only used it twice, when my daughter was getting married and, I had to pay for plane tickets for her husband's extended family."

"But nevertheless, you still introduced Mr Yilmaz to him."

"Yes, Ahmet and I are cousins and came to this country together," he said, with a sad smile on his face, "so, when he told me of his mother's illness, I did everything I could to help, even lent him money."

"Did you know, he was using Cartulary's Hawala bank to transfer money back to Istanbul?"

"Yes, but how much, was between him and Giorgio and now, he is dead and my friend, he has lost his money."

"Well, nothing is certain at this stage Mr Ozdemir and, I would ask you to keep such information to yourself for the time being,' Czerniak said, before asking, "tell me, did you know on what dates he sent the money?"

"No, I'm afraid my only involvement was when, after introducing Ahmet to Giorgio, I took him to that garage in Kinmel Bay."

"When was the last time you were there?"

"On that day, oh, maybe six or seven months ago."

"And, when did you last see the man you know as Giorgio Cartulary?"

"Erm, that is a good question and one, I couldn't answer with any certainty, but it must be five weeks or more since he last came to Friday prayers."

After returning Mr Ozdemir to his Kebab house in Queens Street, Czerniak and Rajni drove to Conwy where, without saying a word, he parked up in one of the narrow side roads.

"Listen," Czerniak suddenly said, after sitting thinking in absolute silence, for about two minutes, "I'm almost certain, that this job is linked to this Hawala bank thing and I urgently need to get my head around it and, there is only one way to do that, which is to talk to someone who knows the ins and outs of it and, isn't afraid to speak."

"In other words, you're asking me to get in touch with my dad."

"Would he talk to me?" He asked, after finally turning the cars' engine off.

"I can ask him," she said, getting out of the car to make the phone call.

Ten minutes later and, after making numerous promises, that he wouldn't disclose anything to Rajni, Czerniak had a full and frank discussion with Mr Latifa.

"Well, what did he have to say," was her first question, when Czerniak returned to the car.

"Erm, that he was proud to hear about your promotion," he replied, turning to put his seat belt on.

"No, you know what I mean, what did he tell you about the Hawala bank?" She asked, her voiced now slightly raised.

"Sorry Rajni, but I promised your dad, that whatever he told me, would stay between him and me," he replied, unconvincingly.

"Yeh, but he's my father, so, surely, he didn't mean me?" She said, now noticeably getting more and more angry.

"In fact," Czerniak added, "he was quite insistent, that you, above everyone else, shouldn't know what he told me."

"That's bollocks and you know it," she said, now barely able to conceal her anger.

"It might well be bollocks, but nevertheless, I made your father a promise and, I'm sticking to it," he said starting the engine, "come on, let's see how the other two have got on."

There journey to St Asaph, along the dual carriageway, may have only taken them twenty minutes but, the ice-cold atmosphere, caused by Rajni's foul mood, made it feel far longer.

"Bloody hell, what's with the long face?" Tony asked, after seeing Rajni, dump her coat and handbag on her desk and storm off to the toilets.

"It's nothing," Czerniak replied, "just a difference of opinion, now then, let me get myself a coffee and then, you can tell me what you've found out about our Mr Sutherland's, alter ego."

By the time Czerniak finished making his coffee, Rajni had returned and, after giving her boss, a fake angry look, she grinned and then, sat next to him.

"Well, now that you two have kissed and made up," Tony said with a broad grin, "let me tell you a story, about a man called Georgio Cartulary."

During the course of the morning, he and Danny had begun the unenviable task, of going through the endless pile of documents, letters and invoices which had been found in Sunderland's safe.

Tony, it seems, had decided to concentrate on anything relating to Georgio Cartulary and, having discovered a birth certificate in that name, checked it, and the passport, found in Sunderland's car, with the Home Office.

Having learnt, that both were genuine, he delved deeper into Cartulary's past history and family.

With the birth certificate, indicating that Georgio had been born in Coventry, to an Italian father and, an Ethiopian mother, Tony had searched the census records, looking for a family, with the surname Cartulary.

With years of experience as a detective behind him, Tony soon traced the family, to a multi-occupancy house, containing on the face of it, mostly immigrant families.

He did however note, with some interest, that one other family name stood out, mostly because, unlike the others, it was Anglicised.

The Sunderland family, had consisted of husband and wife, James and Elaine and, their two children, Marie and Edward.

Disappointed, that the son wasn't called Garry, or even Gareth, Tony explored further into the Sunderland family background and, was surprised to discover, that a third child had died, aged 6 months.

A quick check through the death certificates for that period, revealed that Gareth John Sunderland had died, from sudden infant death, or cot death.

"So, are you saying, that Sunderland's real name is Georgio Cartulary and, for some reason, he reinvented himself, using a dead child's identity?" Czerniak asked.

"Looks that way boss," Tony replied, "and, even though his father, being of Italian descent, was Catholic, his mother was, by all accounts, a practising Muslim."

"Which would explain, his visits to the Mosque in Llandudno," Rajni said.

"Yes, though, I seem to think, he was using his knowledge of that culture, to drum up trade for this Hawala bank of his," Tony replied.

"Hmm, yes, I would tend to agree with you there," Czerniak said, "because we spoke to a guy called Yusuf Ozdemir earlier and he said, that Sunderland, liked to network in the Mosque, after Friday prayers."

"Well, he certainly knew how to keep the two lives separate," Danny declared, as he produced that year's diary, with future dates and events, individually marked out, using either of his two identities.

Knowing, that the real Gareth Sunderland had been born in 1994 and, had died in the same year, Danny had worked backwards, to discover when, Cartulary started to use his name.

The building, containing Sunderland's car showrooms, had been leased from a company, called Blackwall Properties, based in Chester and, according to their estate's manager, for the last five years, there had been no problems, with either their tenant or, his monthly payments.

Thankfully, prior to leasing the property, Blackwall Properties had asked Gary Sunderland for a reference, which it seems, had been provided his former employer, a Mr Giorgio Cartulary, the owner, of Cartulary Motors, based in Telford, Shropshire.

A quick check, revealed that this company had existed for no more than twelve months and, had closed suddenly, with quite a number of clients out of pocket.

Since arriving in North Wales, Sunderland, met, married and divorced his wife Yvonne all within two years and, according to her, was an, habitual liar and cheat, whose only loyalty was to money.

"So, by all accounts, he was an all-round womanising liar and, an out and out, money grabbing shit," Czerniak said, after hearing everything what the two officers had discovered, "and, it looks like he left Telford in a hell of a hurry, with god only knows how many creditors in his wake. Then, as calm as you like, takes on the name of some kid, who died in the same house he was brought up in, gets married and divorced, leaving his wife to bring up their child on her own and then, latches onto our superintendent's wife, presumably, after discovering she was worth a small fortune, question is, who, out of any number of suspects killed him, and then her, into the bargain."

Chapter 10.

With a list, of potential suspects, growing literally by the day, Czerniak tasked Danny with interrogating the mobile phones, owned by Gary Sunderland and Linda Griffiths.

Then, with a wish to eliminate, as many of those suspects as possible from the enquiry, he visited Craig Duffield, a body builder, bouncer and, one-time boyfriend of Linda Griffiths.

To say, that Duffield was belligerent when interviewed, would be a gross understatement and, on several occasions, Czerniak had to warn him about his language and, aggressive behaviour.

Nevertheless, despite desperately wanting, Duffield to become the prime suspect, Czerniak had to eliminate him from the enquiry because, at the time of the murder, the bouncer was being held in police custody, facing charges of assault.

Next on his list, were the twelve creditors, who between them, had lost, an estimated sum, of fifty thousand pounds, when Georgio Cartulary's car showrooms in Telford, ceased trading, almost five years ago.

Consisting mostly of businesses people, who had supplied goods and services to Cartulary, they were spread far and wide, but none the less, the team spent the next three days tracking them all down and, one by one, eliminating them from the enquiry.

Now, into the second week of their investigation and, with the distraction of Cartulary's former collapsed business, now hopefully put to bed, the team, turned their focus, back to the Hawala bank and, any potential aggrieved customers.

This however, proved to be far more difficult than any of them had first imagined because, as many of the customers they approached, had used the Hawala method of money transfer, to avoid any outside or, official scrutiny, they were now, most reluctant to talk to the police.

In the main, the customers, were older men, of middle eastern or Asian descent, who had a natural distrust of officialdom and, in some cases, had previously fallen foul, of the British judiciary system.

With this hurdle to overcome, even before asking any questions, the team, were becoming more and more reliant on Rajni, to either accompany them during an interview or, pave the way beforehand.

However, despite her presence, the more conservative thinking of those customers, were polite, but reluctant to discuss their financial dealings with, or in front of a woman.

"Christ, it's like stepping back into the bloody middle ages," Danny said to Rajni, as they left the interview room, "I mean, all we're asking, is for him to confirm he's done business with Cartulary, not how many women he's shagged."

"It's because of me," she replied, "and, because he's very much like my own father, he believes, that women are inferior and unable to understand, such complex matters."

"I don't give a bloody monkey's what he sodding well believes and, if he doesn't start talking soon, he'll be seeing the inside of a cell," Danny said in total frustration, "I mean, how do you put up with such backward thinking from your own father?"

"It's not his fault, it's just the way their generation were educated and, still are, in places like Afghanistan," She replied, trying her best to calm Danny down, "look, it's all down to the impression you give, so, when we go back in, you take the lead and, after a few minutes, send me out of the room, to get some tea."

"No sarge, it's too bloody demeaning, Christ, this is not the bloody nineteen fifties and I'm certainly no Gene Hunt," he said, referring to the television series, 'Life on Mars.'

"But, if it gets a result."

The ploy worked, but only to the extent, that Iraqi business man they were interviewing, would admit to knowing Georgio Cartulary.

Having agreed, that his telephone number was identical to the one listed under his name in Georgio Cartulary's mobile phone, he denied point blank, that he'd sent money to an Hawala bank in Erbil, Iraq.

"It's no good boss, it's like pulling bloody hen's teeth," Danny said angrily, as he threw the bundle of interview notes onto his desk, "even when the bugger was shown the bloody evidence, he still stared me in the face and denied he'd ever used an Hawala bank to send money abroad."

"Look, we know, those coded messages, relate to an individual's mobile phone number," Czerniak bemoaned, "but, unless these men start talking, we have no way of proving that they actually used the bank and, without that crucial evidence, we may never find a link, to whoever shot the poor buggers."

"Can't we get some form of immunity for them from HMRC," Tony asked.

"Good suggestion," Czerniak replied, "question is, who do we know with enough clout, to swing it for us."

"What about the DCI, he moves in those sorts of circles doesn't he?" Rajni asked, tongue in cheek.

"And, which type of circle are you talking about exactly."

"Well, isn't he on the square, or whatever the expression is," she asked, now looking decidedly embarrassed.

"Are you saying, that Andrews is a bloody mason?" Danny blurted out.

"Well, erm, he is, isn't he," she replied, not knowing if Czerniak was angry or not.

"Look, I've got no idea if he is or not, but I'll run it passed him," Czerniak said, and then after thinking about what he'd just said, added, "that's the suggestion of some sort of pardon for the witnesses, not if he's a bloody mason."

With the tracing and interviewing of former Hawala bank customers, put on temporary hold, Czerniak suggested the team had an early finish.

Then, once the three DCs had left the incident room, Czerniak telephoned DCI Andrews, to discover what progress had been made with Mrs Glendenning.

"Well, knowing it required a very subtle and, sympathetic touch, I went myself in the end," Andrews replied, in a rather modest way, "though I don't know why I bothered, as she was already up in arms, after some, no win, no fee lawyer had rattled her cage."

"Bloody hell, when was that," Czerniak said, trying his best, to sound astounded by the news, whilst at the same time, stifling a fit of laughter.

"Did you know about this?" Andrews suddenly barked, after hearing what he thought was a snigger.

"No boss," Czerniak replied, before pretending to sneeze loudly, in order to hide his laughter, "sorry about that, but this office is so very dusty, so, erm, what did she have to say."

"Hmm," Andrews muttered, still not totally convinced, if Czerniak was taking him for a fool or not, "well, like you said, having been convinced, that this young storeroom assistant or whatever she was, had been stealing from her, Mrs Glendenning sacked her."

"Convinced, by who, did she say?" Czerniak asked, his laughter, now under control.

"Well, that's just it, because according to her, this Jennifer Gibson, was the only person, besides herself, who had legitimate access to the stores at that time, which is why, she's maintaining, that she was justified in sacking her."

"Did you ask, if her husband had access to her workplace?"

"Of course, and, as you might expect, she had a very plausible reason for him visiting the premises, on numerous occasions," Andrews said quietly.

"Christ, come on boss, don't leave me dangling mid-air."

"Well, he was apparently concerned for her welfare, after the premises had been burgled."

"Bit convenient," Czerniak said, whilst pondering the news, "so, was the break in reported?"

"No, because it seems, as it was just a smashed window and, as nothing apparent had been stolen, her husband, persuaded her against involving the police or insurance company, as it would only incur a higher premium."

"The bastard smashed it himself," Czerniak said angrily.

"Exactly what I thought, as it then gave him the perfect cover to come and go at will."

"What about the allegation this Jennifer Gibson made, you know, about him placing the orders and taking the packages directly from the delivery driver."

"No, she wouldn't have any of it and, still believes it was a complete fabrication, you know, to cover the fact, that the young girl had been stealing for months."

"And the fact, that Glendenning and Brooks had been using cyanide to kill people, what did she have to say about that?"

"A pure coincidence."

"Christ is she that bloody naïve?" Czerniak asked, his anger and frustration beginning to raise its head.

"More worried by this unfair dismissal case and what it's going to cost her, because she mentioned, on several occasions, the fact that her ex-husband's lawyers were already costing her a small fortune."

"Out of interest, does her company still use cyanide, as I thought she was more into the digital side?"

"Apparently, when they get in a very old roll of film, they use a miniscule amount, which is rare, and why, they haven't purchased any for about five years."

"But, from what I understood, from the informant, an order for cyanide, was placed quite recently."

"Yes correct, but she's adamant, that it must have been this Gibson girl."

"But for what reason, I mean, except as a poison, it has very little use or worth for that matter."

"Yes, I know, I know," Andrews said frustrated by Czerniak's continued questions, "but unless she changes her mind, were stuck with her explanation."

"What about the delivery driver?"

"Yes, well, I'm ahead of you there," Andrews replied, "because, after leaving her premises I hightailed it across town to Stepney to see the delivery driver, who, without much prompting, confirmed, he handed three packages at least, to a middle-aged man, but unfortunately, he has no idea what was in them but, reckons it was always the same man."

"So, do I take it from that, he only remembers it was a middle-aged man who took delivery of the three packages and, he's no idea who he was."

"Like he says, he drops off hundreds of packages every day, all over London and he's no idea who half the people are who take delivery let alone, what their names are."

"But it definitely wasn't this Gibson girl," Czerniak asked.

"No, just some middle-aged man, though he did describe him as, and I quote, 'very much up himself', which pretty much describes Glendenning I would have thought."

"Yeh, but unless we put him in a line up, we have no way of proving it was him or, for that matter, what was in the packages," Czerniak said

"Exactly, or what dates the deliveries were actually made and, unless Mrs Glendenning plays ball and voluntarily gives us access to her books, then we're up shit creek without a paddle, because we'll never get a warrant," Andrews replied in agreement, "but nevertheless, I've emailed their statements over to CPS, so fingers crossed, they might grow a backbone and try and fight this one."

"Huh! I won't hold my breath," Czerniak said, "anyway, while you're on the line boss, I was wondering, if you had any connections at HMRC."

"Well, if it's got anything to do with not paying tax on your overtime, you can forget it," Andrews said with a slight chuckle.

For the next five minutes, Czerniak briefly outlined the case they were working on in North Wales and, the problems they were having with former customers of Sunderland's Hawala bank.

Fortunately, Andrews claimed to know several influential people, within the upper echelons of His Majesty's Revenue and Customs and, with his promise, to make some enquiries, Czerniak, switched off the lights in the office and headed back to the hotel.

Chapter 11.

As the team, arrived at the incident room the following morning, they were followed in, by a D/I Healy and D/S Brough, from the Regional Crime Squad, who said, they were dealing with a series of robberies from Hawala banks and, were anxious to discover, what progress had been made in their enquiries into Cartulary's money transfer business.

"The simple answer, is none," Czerniak answered cautiously, whilst wondering, how information, he thought was on the need to know basis, had reached the ears of the Regional Crime Squad, based in Chester, "as we seem to be up against this impenetrable wall of silence from his former customers."

"Yes, that's what we initially found," D/I Brian Healy said, with a certain amount of bravado, as he took a seat at one of the vacant desks, "but once the customers we were dealing with, discovered, that because their money had been stolen here in Britain, the transfers hadn't been honoured on the other side, they soon changed their tune."

"How many offences are you dealing with?" Czerniak asked, more out of politeness than anything else.

"Hmm, yeh, good question because, as you no doubt, have already discovered yourself, there is a certain amount of secrecy surrounding that type of business," D/I Healy replied, as he gratefully accepted a cup of coffee from Danny, "cheers mate, but, of those who have come forward, we have six so far, spread over three force areas."

"What level of violence was used?" Rajni asked as she handed a second cup of coffee to D/S Brough, who had decided to sit close to the white board, displaying photographs from their murder scene.

"Yes, well, one elderly chap died after quite a sustained assault, though it is thought it was more to do with an underlying heart condition, than a result of his injuries, but nevertheless, we're treating it as murder," the D/I replied, in a rather off hand manner.

"What about the others?" Czerniak asked, surprised by D/I Healy's, seemingly lack of empathy for the victim, "was anyone shot or, a gun produced?"

"No one shot as yet no," he replied, with a slight cough to clear his throat, "but several of the victims, claimed to have been pistol whipped though, none of them could identify the type of gun used."

"Shit, so, they're not adverse to using violence then."

"No, and with the level of violence increasing on each offence, it's only going to be a matter of time before we have another death on our hands," D/S Brough replied, making it sound as though the victims were to blame in some way.

"So, do you think there's a link between your jobs and ours?" Czerniak asked, now hoping that D/I Healy and his odious sergeant would leave.

"That's what we're here to find out," D/I Healy said, as he walked over to study the murder scene photographs

For the next half hour, the two officers from the Regional Crime Squad, did their best, to dig and probe, as they tried in vain, to discover who Czerniak's main suspects were.

Then, and only after realising, that the information he required, was not going to be forthcoming, D/I Healy eventually told Czerniak, that despite all the offences in Merseyside, Cheshire and Shropshire involving, Hawala banks, none, were linked to Georgio Cartulary or his alias, Garry Sunderland.

He did however disclose, that just like the customers who had used Cartulary's bank, nearly all of the one's he was dealing with, had been sourced, after Friday prayers, in a variety of local Mosques across the region.

With some reluctance, D/I Healy also revealed, that whereas his initial thoughts and suspicions were, that one or more, of those customers were involved, he was now looking elsewhere.

Now, with the exchange of ideas becoming, more and more open, Czerniak revealed for the first time, that despite having a Muslim mother, he didn't wholeheartedly believe, that Cartulary was a true follower of that religion.

This news, prompted D/I Healy to ask what reason, would Georgio Cartulary have, for pretending to be a Muslim.

"Well, like everything else in his life," Czerniak concluded, "Gary Sunderland, seemed to use people and, in this case, he reverted to his given name, just to further his greed."

To further expand on that statement, Czerniak then explained, how Superintendent Griffiths believed, that having discovered he was a wealthy man, Garry Sunderland had targeted him, by beginning a relationship with his wife.

"Why, how much is he worth?" D/I Healy asked.

"Several million I think, and of course, if she'd have gone through with the divorce, then potentially, Sunderland would have had access to at least half of it."

"And, from what you say about his business dealings in Telford, wouldn't have been averse to disappearing with the lot," the D/I said, before pondering for a moment, "tell me Jack, is there any indication, that either the super or his wife, knew about Sunderland's dual identity."

"Well, when we spoke to him originally, John Griffiths seemed totally unaware of Georgio Cartulary and, as there was only one plane ticket to Istanbul, I can only assume, that she had no idea either."

"And the Super's got a cast iron alibi you say?"

"Spent the evening at a do in the local golf club with, our resident Detective Inspector, Mel Jones."

"Mel Jones?"

"Yes, why do you know him?"

"Erm, yes, well, we were on a course at Bramshill together about two months ago, seems a decent enough chap."

"Yes, I got that impression to."

Then, with a promise, to forward on, anything they considered relevant, D/I Healy and D/S Brough left the incident room.

"So, what do you make of that?" Czerniak asked his small team.

"Interesting," Rajni replied, "but only from the point of view, that under normal circumstances, that visit would have been carried out by a couple of D/Cs or at the most, a D/S, but certainly not, a D/I."

"Yeh, it stinks boss," Tony agreed.

"Good to see, you've all got your wits about you this morning and, I take it, you noticed where our faithful D/S Brough, positioned himself to take notes."

"Question is boss," Danny asked, "was he writing down what was being said, or what was on the white board."

"And, why come all the way here from Chester, when a phone call would have sufficed?" Tony added, "yeh, like I said, the whole thing stinks."

"So, my friends, it looks like someone, somewhere, is leaking confidential information about our enquiry, possibly, because they want to manipulate which road we take or, if not, too find out, exactly what we know," Czerniak said, whilst pondering what to say next, "which means, from now on, we tighten our security and, above all else, put a zip on it, you talk to no one, is that clear?"

"Yes boss," was the combined response.

"Now then, I spoke with DCI Andrews last night, about getting some sort of amnesty for the people who used Sunderland's bank and, he's speaking to someone at HMRC later today."

"Well that's good news," Rajni said with a cheeky grin, "and erm, did you ask him about that other matter?"

"What, whether or not to transfer you to the traffic wardens' department," Czerniak replied, with a broad grin, "anyway, while we wait for a result, I need you Tony, to gee up your contact in the Istanbul embassy, to see if the money sent by Mr Yilmaz actually arrived."

"Yeh, on it," Tony replied.

"Which leaves us three, free to bottom out, once and for all, the alibi given by Superintendent Griffiths."

Whilst Czerniak spoke to and then, recorded a written statement from D/I Mel Jones, Rajni interviewed his wife, Jill.

With both, giving an almost verbatim version of the events, of that fateful Friday evening, it was beginning to look that any initial suspicions, that had fallen on Superintendent Griffiths, were lifting.

Their version of events, was also quickly backed up by former architect, Geraint

Edwards, when he was interviewed by Danny Murphy.

However, when Rajni and Czerniak eventually tracked down district nurse, Julia Edwards, they found she was somewhat unsure on several, quite crucial points.

Initially, during their rather informal chat, before commencing a written statement, Mrs Edwards agreed, that John Griffiths had arrived at the golf club at around 8pm however, once she realised, her words were going to be committed to paper and, was told of the consequences if she lied, she began to change her mind.

After originally agreeing, with the general consensus of opinion, decided by all four witnesses, that Superintendent Griffiths had arrived at the golf club on or around 8pm, she now said, it may have been later.

When pressed by Czerniak, to try and give an exact time, Mrs Edwards said, she thought it was sometime after 9.00pm, as she remembered being annoyed by the fact, that halfway through the main course of the meal, she had to move seats to accommodate John Griffiths.

She then went on to say, that due to his dark mood and, lack of interaction with the others, that she and Jill Jones got up to dance, the moment the music started.

Having decided to give John Griffiths a wide berth that night, she and Jill, remained on the dance floor from about 10.00pm onwards and, as such, she was unaware of what time he left the golf club.

Asked, why she and the other three had originally stated, that John Griffiths arrived at around 8.00pm and departed at 1.00am, she declared, that the amount of alcohol, consumed on the night, had clouded their memories.

"It's a bloody cover up," Rajni said, as they left the hospital, where Mrs Edwards worked.

"I agree, so, before they have a chance to talk to each other, let's get the other three back in and, ASAP."

By the time they arrived back in St Asaph, Jill Jones and Geraint Edwards were already ensconced in separate interview rooms and D/I Jones, was pacing up and down in the corridor outside the incident room.

"What the hell, is the meaning of this?" D/I Jones demanded angrily, as soon as he caught sight of Czerniak, "you've dragged my wife and friend in here like some common criminals and, to top it all, have barred me from entering the incident room, I do hope you have an excellent explanation, or I'll see to it, that you and your team, are on the next train, back to London."

"Well, first of all Detective Inspector," Czerniak said, pushing his face as close as he dare to the other mans, "I think any decision, as to whether we remain here or not is down to the Home Office and secondly, you, your wife and friend have been asked to attend the police station to explain, why all three of you, lied on your written statements."

"Lied, why that's tantamount to," he started to say, before Czerniak finished he sentence.

"Perjury, yes Inspector, a criminal offence and, not the type of thing, that you, as a serving police officer, would want on your CV," he said with a sneer, "so, if you wouldn't mind accompanying me into this spare interview room, we can speak with you first."

Having read out aloud, the statement made by Julia Edwards, Czerniak placed it directly in front of D/I Jones and asked him, if he had any comments to make.

"Look, it's true what she said, you know, about him disrupting the main course but, when I asked him why he was late, he said he'd been sat outside in his car for over an hour, trying to decide whether to come in or not."

"And what, you just believed him?" Czerniak asked, incredulous that a Detective Inspector, would just accept such an excuse from a murder suspect without at least verifying it.

"We all did, well, all except for Julia, whose never really liked him for some reason," he replied, shrugging his shoulders.

"And his mood, Mrs Edwards described it as being dark, was she correct about that as well?"

"Yes, well, he certainly wasn't the life and soul of the party if that's what she meant and yes, I suppose he did seem a little down in the mouth."

"Julia Edwards, also said, that from about 10.00pm onwards, she and your wife were on the dancefloor and therefore, they had no idea where Superintendent Griffiths was or even, if he was still in the golf club."

"Erm, yes, as I recollect, Julia got up first and then, about fifteen minutes later she dragged Jill up and erm, yes, I suppose it's fair to say, that they remained on the dance floor until the end of the evening."

"And alcohol, how much would you say you drank personally?'

"Erm, bearing in mind we used a local taxi service that night," he replied before clearing his throat nervously, "erm, I had one or two large G and T's before the meal then, we shared several bottles of wine, plus the one Geraint won on the raffle and, I think we ended the night at the bar, with couple of brandies."

"From what I understand, John wasn't drinking that night, is that right?"

"Yes, that's correct, I think he said, something about the strong sedatives he was on."

"Did you and Geraint dance at all?"

"Well, he's always been one for bopping away, so it was difficult to hold him back, especially after what he'd drunk."

"And what about you," Czerniak persisted.

"Yes, I danced, but not as continuously as the others," he replied rather coyly, "not that I didn't want to, it was, well, as it was me who'd persuaded John to attend the club that night, I thought you know, sort of duty bound, and anyway, he looked so bloody miserable on his own so, despite the groans and complaints from the others, I went back to sit with him a few times."

"So, in other words, for the best part of the night, you and the other three were, to put it in the vernacular, pissed and, having a good time."

"If you like, yes."

"Well, it's how you described it, so, is that a good description of how your evening went."

"Yes, I suppose it is."

"So, if that's the case, how did you know, with any certainty, what time John Griffiths left the golf club?"

"Because, I asked him," he blurted out before saying, in a far more subdued manner, "look, you have to remember, that for one thing, I had the mother of all hangovers and another, the wife of a very good friend, had just been brutally murdered, so yes, I asked him and, to be perfectly honest with you, I believed him."

"So, are you actually telling me, that you asked the prime suspect in a double murder, what time he left the golf club and, because he said it was around 1:00am you believed him?" Czerniak said, in total disbelief.

"Erm, yes, I'm afraid so and, to pre-empt your next question, yes, it was me, who then gave the other three the time line because, to be perfectly honest with you, none of us had a clue."

"Is that because, you were either, all dancing or too drunk to remember seeing him go?"

"I'm afraid the answer to that question, is both." he replied quietly, "but you have to understand, I've known John for years and, I just can't believe he'd have had anything to do with killing either of them."

Chapter 12.

Having been told that her husband had changed, not only his recollections of the events on that fateful night, but also, his written statement, Jill Jones did the same, as did Geraint Edwards.

Despite, originally lying to the police but, mainly because their statements had not been officially submitted into evidence, the CPS decided, that the full offence of perjury had not been committed and therefore, none of them faced any further action.

However, D/I Jones was still a serving police officer and, as he would now be facing an internal disciplinary hearing, he was removed from front line duties and, his position, as liaison between Czerniak's enquiry team and his own force.

That role, was very quickly handed to Martin Jarvis, a rather young and newly promoted Detective Sergeant, who immediately made it known to Czerniak that, whilst not biased in anyway, regarding Superintendent John Griffiths' involvement, he would not be drawn into any form of witch hunt.

It was, on his first morning in the role of liaison officer, that D/S Jarvis brought Czerniak the news, that sometime, during the early hours of the morning, another Hawala bank had been robbed at gunpoint, in a quiet residential area of Flint.

Travelling with Czerniak, to the town of Flint, some twenty miles from Rhyl, D/S Jarvis began to open up about himself and, his ambition to be a D/I before reaching the age of thirty, along with the hope, that his involvement in this enquiry, wouldn't hold back his career in any way.

"So, do I take it from that, you only get involved in open and shut cases?" Czerniak asked rather sarcastically.

"No, far from it," he replied, the sarcastic nature of the question having eluded him totally, "what I'm saying is, that I try my best, to take on tasks, that will, how can I put it, further my career."

"So, you're not a university entrant then?"

"No, which is why, I have to carefully pick and choose and, only take on tasks that will get me noticed," he replied with a smug smile, "like for instance, that recent spate of day time burglaries we were having in and around Rhuddlan."

"Can't say I heard about them," Czerniak said with a shrug of his shoulders.

"Hmm, no, no I don't suppose you would have," he mumbled rather disappointedly, before carrying on regardless, "but, because they involved the homes of a local politician and a solicitor, the burglaries came to the notice of the Chief Constable."

"So, high profile then?" Czerniak said, trying to humour Jarvis.

"Oh yes, very much so and, when I collared the lad and recovered most of the stolen goods, well, you can only imagine the good it did my reputation and of course, ultimately, my career."

Not wanting to hear any more, about how D/S Jarvis was single handily taking on the entire criminal underworld of North Wales, Czerniak asked him, what he knew about Flint, the town they were heading for.

Less than ten miles from the border with England, it was within easy reach of nearby Chester and of course, Liverpool, the source, D/S Jarvis told him, with the authority of someone, with his finger on the pulse, of most of the heroin and crack cocaine, that entered their force area.

Fortunately, D/I Bob Knight, the officer in charge of the robbery case, was far more down to earth than D/S Jarvis and, having been able to free himself of the liaison officer, Czerniak began to look for similarities with the double murder he was investigating.

Almost immediately, Czerniak was drawn to the fact, that at least one of the three offenders were carrying a handgun and, although no firearms were discharged, the victim had believed, his life was in imminent danger

Initially convinced, that his offenders, were somehow known to the victim of the robbery, D/I Knight had commenced his enquiries, by trawling through a list of bank customers, hoping to spot any likely suspects.

However, with the vast majority of those customers, being elderly or, middle aged men, with very conservative religious beliefs he was struggling.

The victim, a Mr Mahmoud, a former Egyptian spice trader, had lived in Flint for over twenty years, where he ran a small convenience store.

It had been, through the contacts he'd made as a spice trader, that Mr Mahmoud had been able to establish his Hawala banking system and, with links, throughout the Middle East, had been operating it for over fifteen years.

As all three offenders had worn, full head masks and gloves, Mr Mahmoud had been unable to identify any of them or, guess at their ethnicity and, with only one of them speaking, very briefly, an accent of any description.

With all other avenues of enquiry, rapidly closing, D/I Knight had already been in touch with D/I Healy at the Regional Crime Squad office in Chester, though like Czerniak, he believed, that the flow of information, was only going in one direction.

"So, have you dealt with D/I Healy in the past?" Czerniak asked, whilst watching Bob Knights face for a reaction.

"Let's just say, our paths have crossed," he replied with a scowl.

"I take it by that, you don't entirely trust him?"

"Look, don't get me wrong, Brian Healy is quite a decent bloke in his way but, he's easily manipulated," the D/I replied, before taking Czerniak to one side, so they wouldn't be overheard, "no, it's that Bloody Clive Brough, I have a problem with."

"In what way?" Czerniak asked, after making sure, that D/S Jarvis was well out of earshot.

"Well, for one thing, I've caught him in here on several occasions, rifling through the lad's trays and files."

"Looking for what exactly?"

"Quick hits, you know, where all the leg work has already been done and all that's left to do, is to go out and lift the offender."

"Oh, you mean he's a glory hunter?" Czerniak said, having finally understood what the D/I was hinting at.

"Yes, exactly, a bit like your running mate over there, as I'm told, that a bit like Brough, he likes to mooch about the office, after everyone else has gone home and then, collar the offender himself."

"Hmm, yes, I got that impression, though he doesn't seem to hide it, in fact, appeared to be quite proud of the fact."

"Some say, he's destined to be a DCI or higher before hitting forty, that is of course, unless someone mixes him a bottle beforehand," the D/I said with a thin smile, "anyway, how are you finding Wales and it's strange ways."

"Much the same as London, but with a different accent," Czerniak replied with a broad grin, happy that he'd found someone he thought he could trust.

Despite the fact, that the victim of the robbery in Flint was targeted, both D/I Knight and Czerniak agreed, that unlike the offence in Rhyl, it lacked any hint of a personal grudge.

D/I Knight, also believed that his offenders were local to Flint, as only someone with a detailed knowledge of the area, would have known of the gated alleyway, used to gain access to the rear of the attacked premises.

Having swopped several ideas and theories, the two men parted company and, along with D/S Jarvis, Czerniak headed back to St Asaph.

It was whilst they were en-route to the incident room, that Czerniak received the news he'd been waiting for, which was, that the HMRC had agreed, not to prosecute any customers of Cartulary's Hawala bank.

Having passed that news onto the team, by the time he arrived back in St Asaph, Tony Smith and Danny Murphy were already speaking to some of Cartulary's former customers.

Over the next few days, the team interviewed, a total of twenty-three men, who at one time or another, had used Cartulary's bank to transfer money abroad.

Whereas some, were making modest, regular monthly payments to help with a relative's education or medical bills, one or two others had only used the system once or, maybe twice, to transfer considerable sums of money, in order to pay for a marriage settlement, or house purchase.

All of the men involved, had been introduced to Cartulary in the Llandudno Mosque, by a third party, who usually, turned out to be another former customer.

However, one name, that cropped up several times was Baris Dogan, a young, Turkish born, on-line retailer from Colwyn Bay.

Specialising in high end watches and, an array of mid-range, lady's jewellery, Dogan operated, out of a converted garage, under his split-level house.

With stunning views, of the sea on one side and a golf course and surrounding countryside on the other, the large detached house, sat at the end of quiet and, very private cul-de-sac.

From the moment he opened the front door, Dogan, was not only evasive, in the way he answered even the simplest of questions, but also, somewhat reluctant to invite Czerniak and Rajni into his home.

"Look Mr Dogan," Czerniak said, with his foot wedged hard, against the base of the door, to prevent Dogan from closing it, "it's really quite simple, we either come in and talk in a civilised manner, or you'll be spending the rest of the day in a police station answering questions."

"But, I have nothing to tell you," he protested, still trying to close the door.

"in that case, it won't take long will it," Czerniak replied, now applying the weight of his shoulder to the door.

"But you can't just force your way into my house without a search warrant," he practically screamed.

"Do we need a search warrant?" Czerniak demanded.

"No, well, what I mean, I have seen how you police act on the television and, how you force your way into someone's house and then, rip it apart," he replied, whilst shaking almost hysterically.

"Mr Dogan, please, calm down. Look, all we want to do, is ask you a few simple questions," Czerniak said, trying his best to sound calm and reassuring, "but your reluctance to speak with us, is making me highly suspicious, that you may have something to hide and, unless you cooperate, I will have no choice, other than to arrest you for obstructing a murder enquiry."

"Murder, I haven't, I mean, what murder," he screamed, whilst once again, trying to push his door shut.

"The murder of a man, you might have known as Georgio Cartulary and, his girlfriend."

"Who?" he replied, now somewhat calmer, whilst at the same time, pretending he had no idea who Czerniak was talking about, though the horrified look on his face, told an entirely different story.

"I'll ask you one more time Mr Dogan, are you going to allow us in?"

"Erm, yes, yes, please come in, please follow me," he replied, wiping away the tears from his face, before making his way up the stairs to a large open plan lounge/dinner, with views out over the bay.

Then, over a hastily made cup of coffee, Dogan told them, that having met Georgio Cartulary at Friday prayers and, as they were more or less, the same age, they became friends.

It was however, some months later, after telling his new friend, he wished to purchase a new car, that he discovered Cartulary's alter ego, Garry Sunderland, was a used car dealer.

As their friendship grew, Cartulary eventually revealed the true reason, why he traded under the name Sunderland and, how he wished he could find a way, to pay off his creditors.

This was also, the period, when Dogan's on-line business was in its infancy and, he was struggling financially.

So, with the friends, both desperately looking, for a more lucrative form of income, they came up with a plan, to start a Hawala bank.

As Dogan's family, were well respected in Istanbul, he had very little trouble in establishing Hawala banking links in that city and, two others in Turkey.

However, as they were new to the business and, lacked any line of credit with those banks, they were forced to use a courier, to carry monies between the two countries

Then, with Dogan, drumming up customers from among the congregation, at his local Mosque, Cartulary set up and ran the Hawala bank, from his car showroom.

With some reluctance, Dogan, then told Czerniak and Rajni that, as he and Cartulary, were desperately short of cash at this time, they occasionally borrowed from the pot of money, which in theory, should have been transferred, on a monthly basis, to a bank in Turkey.

Depending solely, on the good will, his family name bought him with the Turkish Hawala banks, Dogan said, he blamed the delay, in transferring the money they'd borrowed, on the vagaries of the British transport system and, a difficulty, in obtaining trustworthy couriers.

Then, after nearly six months, with his own business on a firm financial footing, Dogan ceased to borrow money and believing, that was the same for his partner, he left the day to day running of the bank to Cartulary.

However, in recent months, through a family friend in Turkey, he learnt, that once again, the monthly courier runs, had been delayed and, in some cases, had not taken place.

When he confronted his partner over these allegations, Cartulary initially denied them, claiming that there must be some mistake or, that the courier must have gone to the wrong address.

However, when pressed, he finally admitted to holding back several transfers, in order to settle a large tax bill for his own business.

He also told Dogan, that some of the money he'd borrowed, should have been transferred to a bank, run by Altan Kaplan, whom he believed, may have had links, to a notorious Turkish gang.

Dogan, went on to say, that after being given, only five days, in which to settle a debt, of twenty-five thousand pounds and, in person, Georgio Cartulary, told him, he had booked himself a flight to Turkey.

In the days leading up to that trip to Turkey, between them, they managed to scrape together, sufficient money to pay off the Turkish gang and, hopefully establish a new contact.

"How much money did he have?" Czerniak asked.

"Erm, well, with the money, from three other Hawala transfers, he was holding back for a week and, the twelve thousand pounds I gave him, he had just under twenty."

"Twenty thousand, but surely, that wouldn't have covered his debt with that Kaplan chap."

"No, which is why, he took out a loan with his own bank, using his house as collateral."

"So, what was the total amount he was going to take out to Turkey?"

"Erm, he told me, he'd managed to raise a total of fifty-eight thousand in cash."

"Was that in pounds Sterling?"

"Yes, because Georgio said, the bank in Turkey preferred to have foreign currency, I think, it was because it's safer."

"And, did you actually see the money?"

"No, because it was all very much last minute."

"So, let me get this straight, you're saying, that between you, you managed to raise a total of fifty-thousand pounds?"

"Yes, that's correct."

"But why did you need so much, I thought you said his debt was twenty-five thousand?"

"Yes, again you are correct," he replied, looking rather nervous, "but, once he'd paid off Mr Kaplan and, broken all ties with his bank, he was hoping to establish a new link in Istanbul and of course, making a substantial deposit with a new bank, would create a good impression and a good line of credit."

"So, do I take it, that he intended carrying that amount of money on his person somehow?"

"Erm, yes, it has always been the way."

"And, because it is illegal to carry more than ten thousand pounds out of the country, without declaring it, I take it, the money would have been concealed somehow?"

"Erm, it is, erm, possible yes, but something I know nothing about, because it was always one of Giorgio's couriers who took the money."

"So, these couriers of his, had taken money to Istanbul before, what about him, had Giorgio ever made the trip?"

"Yes, I believe so."

"You believe?" Czerniak said sharply, "look, you either know or you don't know, which is it?"

"Yes, I mean, Georgio occasionally took the money, but how much and to who I can't say."

"Can't or won't?"

"I can't say, as I left everything to Georgio," he replied, as he began sobbing, "yes, I found the customers in the mosque but, after I made the introductions, I left it to him to deal with them and, had no idea who sent what."

"Who else knew of his plans to travel to Istanbul?" Czerniak asked.

"As far as I know, no one, though, the man he was dealing with there, must have known that Georgio was going there to settle the debt."

"You mean, this Kaplan fella?"

"Again, I can't answer that question, because, I just don't know, who he was actually meeting," he said before pausing, "you see, we may have been very close friends, but in many ways, he kept things from me."

"Secrets you mean?"

"No, no not secrets, just things, you know, to do with the Hawala, hmm, he used to say," he said with a faint smile, "if I didn't know, it wouldn't harm me."

"By that, did he mean, things involving the Hawala bank?"

"Yes, well, I assume so."

"What about his girlfriend?"

"Girlfriend, he had no girlfriend," he replied sharply, before saying, "oh, I'm sorry, of course, you mean Mrs Griffiths, the lady who lived in his house."

"Yes, would she have known what he was doing?"

"Erm, I don't see why," he replied, wiping the tears from his cheeks, "I mean, after all, he would have no reason to discuss such matters with her, as she was just a friend, who was staying with him, because she was going through some problem or other in her marriage."

"So, since his death, has this Mr Kaplan been in touch with you, about his money?"

"Erm, no, which I thought was strange, you know, because he'd only given Georgio five days in which to return the money but, just in case he decided to come to the UK, I have been hiding here, keeping out of sight."

"Why, do you think they might blame you for the debt?"

"Erm, well, it was my families name that helped us set up those links in Turkey, so, I can only imagine, that he might believe I was somehow involved."

"Does he know Georgio and Mrs Griffiths were killed?'

"To be honest, I don't know, though I did send a copy of the local newspaper to Mr Kaplan's bank in Istanbul, but I suppose, because Georgio had lied to them, so many times in the past, they might not believe it."

Chapter 13.

With the Turkish police, running background checks on Altan Kaplan and, a gang known as, the Arifs, Czerniak called in a favour with Dave Chisolm, an old friend, now working in the counter terrorism department, in London.

According to Chisolm who, prior to taking up his current post, had spent ten, long years, monitoring the rise of gun crime amongst the capitols' gangs, the Arifs, were well known in the criminal underworld.

With their main source of income, now coming, from drug dealing and extortion, the original gang members, weren't averse, to committing the odd armed robbery or, when the need arose, shooting a rival.

Consisting mostly, of Turkish Cypriot immigrants, the Arifs rose to almost untouchable status after the decline of the Krays however, in the early 2000s, having already established a reputation, for extreme violence, they began to diversify, into money lending and nightclubs.

When asked about Altan Kaplan, Chisolm said he had no knowledge of the man although, he did know of an Ahmet Kaplan, who ran an escort agency, out of an office block in Catford.

Then later, when asked, if he thought that Ahmet Kaplan was capable of a double murder, Chisolm said he was doubtful, as the man, was only thought to have a tenuous link to the Arifs plus, he was well into his seventies.

Having discovered, that the surname Kaplan, was quite common in Turkey and Cyprus, Czerniak was beginning to have serious doubts as to whether the man from Catford was related to the gang member in Istanbul.

This line of enquiry was dealt a further blow, when a police captain, from the Turkish police, telephoned to say, he could find no trace of an Altan Kaplan or, anyone who had links to the Arifs and, despite having supplied him with an address in Istanbul, he also claimed, to know nothing about the supposed Hawala bank, which had allegedly, been receiving money transfers from Georgio Cartulary.

"Well, he's either the most incompetent copper in Turkey or, someone's lined his pockets," Czerniak said when he heard the news.

"Yeh, I agree, it does stink a bit," Tony said, "anyway, what's your opinion of this Dogan character?"

"Hmm, what can I say because, to be honest, I can't make him out," Czerniak replied, "and, if I was pushed, I'd say, he's either a poor liar or, if not, very naïve and, Sunderland took advantage and strung him along for months, in fact, right up until the moment he was killed."

"So, what, do you think boss, that Sunderland lied to Dogan, about owing all that money?" Rajni asked.

"Hmm, well, if what Dogan says is right, Sunderland was gathering together a little nest egg and, from what little I've learnt so far, about our car dealer, I would say, he was a lying, conniving two faced individual, who would have sold his own grandmas teeth, if it meant getting himself out of a hole, question is, how big was the hole?" Czerniak replied, "because, the more I think about it, the more I beieve, this was an organised hit and Mrs

Griffiths, was in the wrong place at the wrong time."

"So, do you think, the fact, that he was shot once in the head, points more, towards it being some sort of execution," Tony asked, "and she, was basically wounded, but unfortunately died from her injuries."

"Yes, something like that or, she tried to intervene and got shot for her trouble. But with regards to him, I think, it was, like you say, very much an execution style killing," Czerniak replied, as he got up to look at the murder scene photographs, "the question is of course, who did it, because from what we've uncovered so far, he'd pissed off, more than one or two serious people."

"So, do you really think it was a professional hit," Danny asked.

"Well, unless anyone else has a better suggestion, I'd say yes because, for one thing, we know the killer, was armed with a gun, which means, he obviously went there, prepared to kill or, at the very least do some serious harm, to one or both of them," Czerniak replied, "and, if he really exists, my money is on this Kaplan guy. So, let's ignore our friendly

Turkish copper, who said he couldn't find him and, look at flights to the UK from Istanbul, preferably to somewhere like Manchester or Liverpool."

"I can do that boss," Tony said, turning to face his laptop computer, "what you after, lone males, arriving just before the shooting and departing, the following day."

"Yes, something like that, but don't make the time scale quite so narrow, as the shooter might be laying low somewhere local," he replied, before turning to the other two, "right, in the meantime, you two have a word with force intelligence and our friend D/I Healy, just in case, we have any home grown hit men, living on the patch."

With his team, busy on their telephones, Czerniak headed out of the incident room and, made his way to Superintendent Griffith's office.

"Ah, D/I Czerniak, yes, come in," the superintendent said with a weak smile, "what can I do for you?"

"It's a bit of a difficult question sir," Czerniak began, as he made his way further into the office, "and, if you feel I'm delving too deeply, please tell me to stop and I'll go no further."

"Hmm, yes, I wondered when you'd want to come and rake through the dirty linen," he said, pointing towards a chair, "take a seat and ask your questions, I've got nothing left of my dignity anyway."

"Well, before I begin sir, I think I should tell you, that having spoken to a number of officers within your force, you, and your reputation, is still held in high esteem."

"That's very good of you to say that, but nevertheless, I know, in my heart of hearts what sort of fool I've been," he replied, before pondering what he'd said for a moment, "hmm, yes, and like they say, there's no fool, like an old one and, I'm certainly feeling my bloody age, I can tell you."

"If I can begin with the day, you and your wife visited Sunderland's car showroom," Czerniak said, trying to move the conversation on, "was that the first time, either of you had met him?"

"Erm, well, I can't speak for Linda of course, but, no, I'd met him twice before," he replied, "and both times, in the showroom."

"Was that in connection, with the purchase of that Mazda?"

"Yes, well, things hadn't been going well between us for a few months and, like I told you, when we spoke previously, I had been looking for a sporty run around for Linda's birthday and, you know, to try and cheer her up and, as I was passing, I called in to see what he had in stock."

"So, any conversation you had with Gary Sunderland, would only have been about you wanting to buy a car?"

"Erm, yes, I mean, on the first occasion, I don't know that we even had, what you might call a conversation, you know, he might have asked what I was after and, as I really didn't know at the time, I just mooched around, looking at the various cars, without really saying anything."

"And, on the second occasion?"

"Yes, well, that must have been a few weeks later, by which time I had more of an idea what I was looking for," he replied with a shrug of his shoulders and, a glimmer of a smile, "and, I must admit, he was very helpful, and told me, he had just purchased, two sports cars, which would be arriving in the showroom the following week. So, I gave him my details and, he promised to phone me when the vehicles arrived."

"So, you say, you gave him your details, does that mean, he also knew what you did for a living?"

"Well, as I was in full uniform on both occasions, I'd say yes, there was a very strong possibility that he did."

"So, knowing your name, rank and occupation, it wouldn't have been too difficult for him, to find out everything he wanted to know about you?"

"No, I don't suppose it would, Christ almighty, you don't think, he found out about the inheritance, before we went to buy that bloody car," he gasped in shock, "and, and, what, he targeted Linda from the outset?"

"I'm afraid, there is a strong possibility, yes."

"The bastard, the absolute bastard," he said, slamming his hand down, hard on the desk top.

"Now sir, I'd like you to think hard, was there any indication, that Linda and Sunderland knew each other, before the day you went to purchase the car."

"Well, if there was, I never saw it, in fact, thinking back to that day, initially, she seemed to be a little dismissive of him and his showroom."

"Oh, in what way?"

"Erm, well, for one thing, I think she said something like, it being a bit of a back street or, shady car dealership," he said with a wry smile, "because, when it came to tradesmen in general, despite her background, Linda, was very much, the quintessential snob."

"So, if that's the case, how did he manage to win her over?"

"Well, for one thing, by bowing and scraping and falling over backwards to be the ultimate charmer," he replied, his earlier smile now a scowl, "because, god only knows, how many times he complimented her on her hair and nails and, helped her in and out of the various cars, before telling her how stunning she looked in the Mazda, especially, as the red paintwork matched her lipstick."

"Jesus, that's creepy."

"Which is what I thought but, Linda being Linda, of course, lapped it up."

"So, despite the fact that you were present, from day one, he made it obvious, to Linda at least, how he felt about her?"

"It was as though I didn't exist."

"Did you say anything?"

"Not at the time no, well, I didn't want to cause a scene but, on the way home, I did mention it yes."

"And what did she say?"

"Well, she agreed that he may have been a little over the top but, on the other hand, she thought he was very charming and, bloody cute."

"Cute?"

"Yes, cute."

"How long after that, did you actually take possession of the Mazda?"

"Two days later, when he delivered it and, suggested, that Linda run him back to the showroom in it, so he could iron out any problems she might have with the car."

"Bit of an odd arrangement."

"That's what I said when I found out, you see, I was in work on that day and didn't know anything about it until later."

"And you said, when we first spoke, that he then began making phone calls to the house and in fact, on one occasion, turned up on your driveway."

"Yes, which, according to Linda, was when it all began."

"But you didn't believe her?"

"Look Inspector, I know, that many of my colleagues thought I was naïve when I married Linda, but the truth of the matter is, I knew about her reputation long before I met her and, well, I was flattered by her attention and, after the sadness and misery of the previous years, I enjoyed her youthful zest for life, but most of all, her company."

"Did you ever meet anyone else at the showrooms?"

"Sorry, how do you mean, someone else?"

"Another member of staff maybe or, a business partner."

"Erm, no, not that I recall, though, I think there were other customers there when I first visited, but I can't be certain."

"And you knew him by what name?"

"Sunderland do you mean?"

"Yes sir."

"Well yes, his name was Sunderland, Garry Sunderland."

"And, before I ask this next question, I know, as you do, that it is an offence to use the PNC for any purpose, other than police business," Czerniak said, before giving the superintendent a knowing look, "so, can I ask you, did you use some other methods of finding out, all you could about Garry Sunderland."

"What, oh yes, I see, hmm, well, of course, I asked around, you know, one or two of my old informants," he replied, "and, from what I could gather, he was not known to the police, or, should I say, had no previous convictions and, from what I could gather, ran, a legitimate business."

"Have you ever heard of Georgio Cartulary?"

"Yes, well, when you asked me previously, I'd never heard of him but, I'd be lying if I said I hadn't, because it's now, very well known, that a passport, in that name was found in Sunderland's car."

"But, do you know who he is?"

"No idea I'm afraid, just that a passport in that name was found in Sunderland's car."

"And, what if I was to tell you, that Cartulary ran a car showroom business in Kinmel Bay."

"Yes, well, I did hear on the grapevine that Sunderland's photograph was inside that passport, so, what are you saying, that he was using a false id?"

"No superintendent, what I'm saying is, that the man you knew as Gary Sunderland, was in fact, Georgio Cartulary's," Czerniak replied, "you see, after his car business in Telford went bust, with huge, outstanding debts, he disappeared and, later re-emerged in Kinmel Bay, using the name Sunderland."

"Just a minute, I'm a little bit confused here," Superintendent Griffiths said, "are you saying, the name Garry Sunderland used, was what, just a pseudonym and, that in reality he never actually existed?"

"Well, the real Gary Sunderland did exist once, but only for a few months," Czerniak replied, slowly, so that the Superintendent could fully understand, "you see, Georgio Cartulary took the name of a child that died, many years ago."

"Jesus Christ," Superintendent Griffiths said quietly, "is this bloody nightmare going to go on forever, I mean, was there no end to that man's deception and lies?"

Chapter 14.

When Czerniak, returned to the incident room, Tony and Danny were both, still busy on their telephones but, there was no sign of Rajni.

"Where's Rajni?" he asked, as he made himself a cup of coffee.

"Erm, too be honest, I've no idea boss," Tony replied, as he ended his phone conversation, "she was here about an hour ago, maybe Danny knows."

"Knows what?" Danny asked, putting his hand over the mouthpiece of his phone.

"Where Rajni is," Czerniak said.

"Didn't she go out about an hour ago," he replied, whilst casting a glance over at Tony.

"That's what I said, but I've got no idea where."

"It's okay," Czerniak said, taking a mobile phone out of his jacket pocket, "I'll give her a bell."

Having tried Rajni's mobile phone three times and only getting through to her answering service, he sent a text message, asking where she was.

"Right then, I'll have to bring Rajni up to date later," he said taking a seat next to Danny, "so, I've had another word with Superintendent Griffiths and, from what he says, it looks very much, like Gary Sunderland, targeted Mrs Griffiths from the outset."

"What, because he'd found out about the late Mrs Griffiths and her inheritance?" Tony asked.

"Yes, I think so because, prior to buying his wife that Mazda, the super had been to the car showroom, on two separate occasions and, not only was he in full uniform, but he gave Sunderland his personal details."

"So, the little bastard did some digging and, hey presto, found out about the dosh and, when Linda Griffiths turns up to look at the Mazda, Sunderland puts the charm machine into overload, and wham, she was hooked," Tony added.

"Looks that way, because, from what we've been told about him, he seems to have been driven by one thing and, one thing only, greed," Czerniak replied, "anyway, how have you two got on chasing, potential hit men?"

Out of the dozen or more flights, arriving at Manchester airport from Turkey, only two had single males on their manifest and, as one was well into his seventies and the other, a teenage boy, Tony had dismissed them from the enquiry.

With no flights, with a Turkish connection, in or out Liverpool, he had then widened his search to cover the East Midlands airport and, with no luck there either, was about to look at the three London airports.

Danny hadn't faired any better either and, having been given the brush off by D/S Brough, who had basically said, he couldn't disclose such sensitive information, he was left with trawling the force intelligence network, as he tried to find a potential, home grown hitman.

He'd also drawn a blank, with regards to the seven phone calls, Sunderland had received on his mobile phone, on the day of his murder.

"All of them, were from the same, unregistered pay as you go mobile," he told

Czerniak, "the same one, that had been sending him text messages for over two months."

"Anything of interest in the messages?"

"Other than 'I love you,' or 'missing you', no."

"Jesus Christ, so are you saying, the bastard had another bloody woman on the go," Czerniak exclaimed.

"Looks that way boss, anyway, I'm hoping for a result from Vodaphone, to see what masts the unknown phone was using."

"Good work you two."

As Danny and Tony, returned to their telephone enquiries, Czerniak picked up his mobile phone and, was about call Rajni when, much to his surprise, D/I Mel Jones entered the incident room.

"Look, I don't wish to be rude Mel, but under the circumstances, I don't think it's appropriate for you to be in here," Czerniak said, as he took the D/I by the arm and walked him out of the room.

"No, I know that Jack, but if, erm, I could have a private word, perhaps in my car, I would be very grateful," he replied, looking extremely tense and nervous.

"This is all a bit cloak and dagger, isn't it?" Czerniak said, as D/I Jones drove them along a narrow country lane, which eventually ended, in a small copse of ash trees.

"Yes, but, I'm afraid with everything that's going on at the moment, it's very necessary," he replied, as he parked up, amongst the trees.

"Do you want to check that I'm not wearing any listening devices," Czerniak asked rather sarcastically.

"No, no that won't be necessary," he replied, without realising that Czerniak had just been sarcastic to him.

"So, what's it all about?"

"Look, I know, that you and your team, are concentrating solely on the murders, but can I ask, are you also monitoring the other, day to day events, that are erm, going on in the force area?"

"Like what?" Czerniak asked, curious to know more.

"Like for instance, any other sudden deaths."

"The plain answer is no, because, to be perfectly honest with you Mel, unless it's flagged up, as being linked to the two murders, then I don't think it falls within our current,

Home Office remit, why, has something happened, I should know about?"

"Well, how can I explain, without sounding neurotic or pathetic," he replied, whilst at the same time, scanning the small wooded area looking for anyone else, "erm, you see, I was more than a little embarrassed, you know, by the fact that I'd been caught out, in my vain attempt to cover for John and, even more so, that I've been replaced, as your liaison officer by, of all people, D/S Jarvis."

"Yes, I can imagine you were but, that doesn't explain why we're here, in these woods."

"Christ, yes, it is rather odd isn't it," he said, with a nervous grin.

"So, come on Mel, what is all this about?" Czerniak asked again.

"Erm, yes, sorry, erm, well, to begin with, let me tell you about Jimmy Hinchcliffe, a career criminal, with a record as long, as the proverbial arm," he said, now sounding a little more relaxed. "Now, Jimmy had lived in the area, for most of his life and, because of his persistent offending, was of course, known to most of us, including John Griffiths, who would use him from time to time, as an informant."

"You used the past tense just then, so, do I take it he's no longer with us?"

"Correct, in fact, he was found dead in his flat two days ago."

"Any suspicion of foul play?"

"Not that we know of at this present time and, from what I can gather, it sounds like, a heroin overdose."

"Was he a known user?"

"I think so, but there was never a suggestion he was, what you might term a hardened addict, or, for that matter, liable to take, a self - inflicted overdose."

"So, I take it, you suspect, it might not be self-inflicted."

"Yes, I'm afraid I do, but first, let me give you a bit of background information and then, you can draw your own conclusions," he replied, before yet again, quickly scanning the woods. "You see, despite attempts by various other officers over the years, the only person, Jimmy would really talk to, was John Griffiths and, I think it's fair to say, he supplied him with some pretty good information and, helped put away some tasty villains."

"Okay, so, where are you going with this?"

"Well, as you know, there was no CCTV at the golf club and so, I had to rely on John's account, of when he arrived and left that night," he said, looking a little embarrassed. "Anyway, enough of the excuses, so, when I heard that Jimmy had been found dead, with just over two thousand pounds, stuffed inside his mattress, I decided to look for cameras, in the vicinity of his address."

"Can I ask, where is this going?"

"Look, please hear me out, because, when I heard of Jimmy's death, I thought, because of their long association together, that it was, you know, only right that I informed John about it. However, when I told him, he reacted, in what I can only call, a very hostile manner and, practically accused me of trying to link him, in some way, to Jimmy's death."

"How bizarre, unless, of course, he had something to do with it."

"That's what I thought, so, having remembered, that following a spate of burglaries at their premises, a local garage, called Threeways, had installed cameras looking out over the roadway that leads to Jimmy's flat, I went and viewed their CCTV."

"For when exactly?"

"Hmm, I can see why they rate you so highly," Mel said with a faint smile, "yes, initially, for the Friday, the night of the murders."

"And, what did you see?"

"At exactly eleven fifteen, a full hour and three quarters, before he said he left the golf club, John Griffiths can be seen, quite clearly, driving his Volvo in the general direction of Jimmy's flat," he said quietly, "and then, twenty-five minutes later, going back towards the golf club."

"But not in the direction of the murder scene."

"No, though, because the garage sits just opposite a roundabout, the same camera, did pick him up, just after one, going in the general direction of Rhyl and of course, the murder scene."

"So, what do you think he was up to."

"Well, one thing I haven't told you yet, is about Jimmy's conviction for manslaughter."

"And, don't tell me, John Griffiths was the officer who dealt with him."

"Yes," he replied, "now then, I wasn't around at that time but, from talking to one or two of the lads who were, they were all surprised, that Jimmy was never charged with murder."

"So, is there some suggestion, that John Griffiths pulled some strings or, maybe, made some evidence disappear?"

"Not that I know of, though somebody did mention the fact, that two eye witnesses, did a bunk to Ireland just before the trial."

"So, let me get this straight, you think that John Griffiths went around to see Jimmy on that Friday night and what, paid him two grand or, called in a favour, but either way, got him to go and shoot Sunderland and Jane Griffiths."

"In a nutshell, yes."

"And Jimmy's death?"

"A bit too coincidental for me, which is why I've asked for an invasive post mortem."

"Are you saying, that you think, John Griffiths had something to do with his death too?"

"Well, what about this for a scenario," Mel said, "John called in a favour and, knowing he had the perfect alibi, persuaded Jimmy to kill

Sunderland and his wife, but then, perhaps, Jimmy decided to blackmail him and so, to silence his one-time informant, he gives him a drug overdose."

"Jesus, that's one hell of an assumption, have you got anything, other than the CCTV from that Friday night."

"Hmm, yes, well, how damming it is, I don't really know but, after seeing him drive down that road on the Friday night, I then trawled the same CCTV system for the day, before Jimmy's body was found."

"And?"

"And, just as it was going dark, a Volvo, identical to John's, was driven passed the garage, heading towards Jimmy's flat but, because the driver was wearing a scarf around the lower part of his face and the registration number was obscured with mud or something, I couldn't say one hundred per cent it was him."

"Did he come back?"

"Well that's just it because, despite watching all of the footage, for the rest of that night, I never saw the car again."

"I take it, if it was him, there are other routes he could have used?"

"Erm, yes, three or four."

"And, you have no concrete proof, that on either of those two nights, John Griffiths actually visited Jimmy's flat."

"No, just that he was going in that general direction."

Chapter 15.

As he returned to the incident room, Czerniak was still mulling over the strange encounter he'd just had with D/I Jones when an almost jubilant Danny almost ran into him.

"Sorry boss, I was just coming to find you," he yelled, like some excited child.

"For Christ's sake Danny, calm down," Czerniak grumbled, as he pushed passed Danny to get into the room.

"Well, whoever, our mystery woman is, she lives, somewhere between Colwyn Bay and a place called Llysfaen," he said, waving his notes in the air, "and, the interesting thing is, her phone hasn't been used, since the night of the murders."

"But, you still don't know who she is though?" Czerniak replied, almost dismissively, "look, I'm sorry Danny, but, we need to shelve everything else for the time being and, concentrate all our efforts on Superintendent

John Griffiths and, his connections, with a prolific thief, called Jimmy Hinchcliffe."

After outlining, everything D/I Mel Jones had told him, Czerniak tasked Danny, with the delicate job of accessing the Superintendents' phone logs and Tony, with finding out, everything there was to know about Jimmy Hinchcliffe, especially the case, where he was convicted of manslaughter.

"And, where the hell is Rajni?" Czerniak demanded, as he began making a written entry, of all the information he'd just been given, into the major incident log book.

"Gone to Chester apparently," Tony replied, as he began accessing Hinchcliffe's list of previous conviction on the computer, "something about wanting to clear up some ambiguities with Sunderland's ex-wife."

"What bloody ambiguities?"

"Couldn't tell you boss, she had a bad reception on her phone."

"Bloody hell, we need her here now, not running around the sodding country, can one of you give her a ring."

"Will do," Tony replied, picking up his mobile, 'no, just going to voice mail boss."

"Okay."

By the time Czerniak had written a full precis, of his conversation with D/I Jones, Tony had downloaded a list of Hinchcliffe's previous convictions.

"Jesus Christ, he was a one-man crime wave," Czerniak said, as he began reading through the earliest part of Hinchcliffe's previous convictions.

"And, from what I can gather, was still very active, right up to his death," Tony replied, handing Czerniak a bundle of intelligence sheets, "seems, he was odds on favourite for that spate of burglaries in Kinmel Bay too."

"Which means, it could have been him who broke into the car showroom."

"Well, it fits his M.O. boss, even down to using bleach to wash away any DNA."

"So, the question is, if Hinchcliffe broke into the showrooms, were the other burglaries part of this so-called spate or, was it committed, in order to make us think it was and, not linked to the murders."

"And what about the stolen cars?" Tony asked, "do you think, it was taken and dumped well off the patch, just to make it look like, it was some scally's from Liverpool."

"Well, it's certainly a good scenario."

"Was he bright enough to think like that though."

"Don't know about him, but John Griffiths, our Superintendent certainly is."

"Do you really think he's been playing us boss?"

"No, not us, me," Czerniak replied, "and, there's only one way to find out for sure, we have to formally interview him under caution."

Following a lengthy phone call with his contact at the Home Office, Czerniak telephoned the force Professional Standards office and spoke, with Chief Superintendent James Cooke.

Knowing, that a serving police officer, could not be interviewed under caution about an alleged criminal offence, by an officer, below his or her rank, Czerniak was forced to ask Chief Superintendent Cooke, to take the lead.

However, it was very obvious from the very outset, that Chief Superintendent Cooke, viewed the evidence against his long-time friend and colleague, as sketchy and circumstantial and, he made no effort to disguise those opinions.

"Is this all you have," he said, after reading a precis of Czerniak's interview package, "I mean, this is just a load of wild speculation and, without one piece of hard evidence to substantiate any of your theory, I can't see how we could even have the audacity to ask Superintendent Griffiths to attend an interview."

"To be honest with you sir, I wasn't going to politely ask, as I was thinking of either formerly inviting him in, if not, arresting him, as I think there's more to our Superintendent Griffiths, than he's letting on."

With the full backing of the Home Office, who had expressed a wish, to have him resolve the case quickly, Czerniak held sway over Chief Superintendent Cooke and, later that same day they interviewed John Griffiths, in the presence of a solicitor.

Following his initial reluctance, to explain how his Volvo car was seen travelling towards Hinchcliffe's home when, he was allegedly in the golf club, John Griffiths eventually burst into tears and, whilst sobbing uncontrollably told them, of the deep depression and suicidal thoughts he'd suffered in recent weeks.

He also told them, that having arrived at the golf club that evening, in plenty of time for the meal, a panic attack had prevented him from leaving his vehicle for almost an hour.

Then, when he did finally pluck up the courage to enter the clubhouse, the disdain on Jill Jones's face, told him, he was most unwelcome.

His discomfort, was only heightened when Julia Edwards, in what he described, as a fit of pique, turned to her husband and declared, she wasn't going to allow, 'a miserable old fart spoil her evening.'

Geraint Edwards, had tried to apologise on behalf of his wife but, because he was now quite drunk and, very possibly, agreed with her opinions, he didn't make a very good job of it and, out of embarrassment, he and Mel Jones had gone off to the bar.

Alone, depressed and dejected, John Griffiths had initially headed for the gents' toilets however, as he reached the doorway, he turned towards a fire-door and left the clubhouse.

For about ten or fifteen minutes, he walked around the carpark, before eventually jumping into his car and driving off.

With no idea where he was headed, John Griffiths said, he drove towards the nearby beach at Pensarn, just under half a mile from the clubhouse.

He agreed, that the route, would have taken him directly passed the flat occupied by Hinchcliffe however, he denied stopping there, claiming instead, to have driven to the beach, parked up and then, walked down to the waters' edge.

Once again, he said, he had strong suicidal thoughts and, at one stage, considered wading out into the sea, to drown himself.

However, just as he was walking into the water, he was disturbed by the laughter of a young couple and, instead of going any further, hurried back to his car.

Now, with his feet very cold and wet, he returned to the golf club, where he sat alone, watching his friends enjoying their night until, eventually he could stand it no longer and so, fully intent on finding his wife and, resolving their differences, he left.

"So, are you saying, that on that Friday night, you drove passed the flat of Mr Hinchcliffe and, that you never stopped or went in."

"Correct, in fact, if truth be told, I can't remember the last time we spoke."

"Is it true, he was your informant?" Czerniak asked.

"Yes, he was."

"And, is it also true, that he had a conviction for manslaughter."

"Yes."

"Can I ask where this line of questioning is going Inspector," Chief Superintendent Cooke said, interrupting Czerniak, in a rather irritable manner.

"And, is it also true, that you spirited away, two vital witnesses in the case, so any hope of a conviction for murder was dropped?" Czerniak asked, ignoring Chief Superintendent Cooke's question.

"Right, that's enough Inspector, outside now," Chief Superintendent Cooke bellowed as he got to his feet.

"No James, he has every right to ask his questions," John Griffiths said quietly, "and, the simple answer is, no, no, I did not spirit them away, though, if truth be known, we did very little to protect them."

"Jesus Christ John, this conversation, is being bloody well recorded," Chief Superintendent Cooke yelled, "just take a minute and think what you're saying and who, you're implicating."

"Thank you, James, but this has gone on far too long," John Griffiths said, indicating with his hand, that the Chief Superintendent should sit down, "yes, I personally, could have done, much, much more, to protect the Riley's, but they were scum and, cut from the same mould as Jim Finnegan."

"I take it, this Finnegan character was the person killed?" Czerniak asked.

"Yes, and, like the Riley's, he was part of a group of Irish travellers, who'd set up home on waste ground in Kinmel Bay."

"An unofficial site, which caused no end of trouble in the local community," Chief Superintendent Cooke added.

"In what way?" Czerniak asked.

"In every way possible," the Chief Superintendent replied, "why, from the very moment they arrived, the burglary rate went through the roof, not to mention the assaults and of course, the rape."

"Rape?"

"Yes, erm, perhaps I should explain from here," John Griffiths said, much to the visible annoyance of Chief Superintendent Cooke, "Gemma Watkins, a fourteen-year-old schoolgirl, was walking home from the local youth club, when she was grabbed off the street and bundled into the back of a white transit van. But, despite being badly beaten and raped, she still managed to give a half decent description of her attacker but crucially, the fact that he had a very distinctive tattoo on the side of his neck."

"I take it, that Finnegan had the same one?"

"Yes, more or less identical however, when James and I went to arrest him, the Riley's immediately came forward and swore blind, that he had been with them in Shotton at the time of the incident."

"Sorry, when you say James, do you mean, Chief Superintendent Cooke here?"

"Yes, I was D/I in Abergele at the time and he was my DCI in Llandudno."

"And Shotton, where's that?" Czerniak asked.

"Oh, sorry, yes, it's a town, about twenty miles away, in the direction of Liverpool."

"Did you believe them?"

"Not at first no, but when they said, he had been helping them strip the lead from a church roof, something Finnegan had form for, the custody sergeant insisted on releasing him on bail for our case and of course, then re-arresting him for the theft."

"So, what happened then?"

"Well, when we discovered that the theft of lead had been reported, we had to rethink our strategy."

"Is this where Hinchcliffe comes into the story?"

"Correct, because I already knew, Jimmy had been doing business with the Riley's."

"Business?"

"Buying and selling mostly," Griffiths replied coyly.

"Look Inspector," Chief Superintendent Cooke said, interrupting the flow of questions once again, "surely, you must know how these things work because, for any informant to be worth his salt, you have to allow them a certain amount of leeway."

"So, in order to get to the bigger prize, you're saying, you turned a blind eye to some petty pilfering."

"John, I must insist that you take time, to carefully think of your answers," James Cooke said, the urgency in his voice all too apparent.

"No, I'm sorry James, I have to clear my conscience because, some of his crimes were not so petty, though, as you say, that's for another day," he replied, giving the Chief Superintendent a knowing look, "anyway, to get back to the case in hand, I tasked Jimmy with getting closer to the Riley's, hoping that they would let something slip, about the night of the rape."

"And did they?"

"Unfortunately for him, Jimmy got sloppy and, one night, he tried to get Billy Riley drunk, but he must have suspected he was up to something because, Riley recorded their conversation, which of course, he later played back to Finnegan," Griffiths said, before pausing for a moment.

"Are you okay to carry on sir?" Czerniak asked.

"Erm yes, it's just that, it was that recording which got Finnegan killed and Jimmy, a prison sentence and of course, indirectly, I suppose, it was our fault."

"I must insist, that you say no more on the subject John, as you're implicating yourself in something you had no part in," Chief Superintendent Cooke said, before turning to the solicitor, "surely, you should be advising your client of his current situation."

"No James, Finnegan may have been an out and out bastard, but like everyone else, he deserved his day in court and, we owed it to Gemma Watkins, to do the right thing," Griffiths said quietly, "and what we did, was unforgiveable."

"What was it, that you did?"

"I think this line of questioning is out of order Inspector," the solicitor suddenly said, "so, can I suggest you move on or, we will be forced to leave, as after all, my client is here voluntarily."

"Hmm, can you at least, tell me what happened to Finnegan?" Czerniak asked, ignoring the scowl on Chief Superintendent Cooke's face.

"Yes, well, erm, like I said, Jimmy had no idea, you know, that Finnegan was on to him, which is why he agreed to go, with him and Billy Riley, to break into Nanerch Hall."

"What's that, a local stately home?"

"At one time maybe, but now its home to a rather insalubrious crime family, called the Grimes," he replied, with a faint smile, "anyway, Finnegan, persuaded Jimmy that there was a pot of money there, just waiting to be snatched and, Jimmy being Jimmy, well, he couldn't resist."

"Were the Grimes family involved?"

"Can't say for certain, as everyone one of them, including their lawyer, was in the Gran Canaries at the time."

"Pretty tight alibi then?"

"Yes, exactly, anyway, it was only after they'd broken into the property and Billy Riley tried to grab him, that Jimmy realised he'd been set up."

"I take it they were going try and pin the job on Jimmy?"

"No one knows for certain, what their intentions were, but Jimmy was far too strong for young Billy Riley and, having relieved him of his cosh, he knocked him to the floor and went for Finnegan with it."

"What, and bludgeoned him to death?"

"No, because that's the strange thing in all of this, as he was stabbed in the back and, the only DNA on the knife, belonged to Susan Riley, Billy's wife."

"Was she there that night?"

"No, and both Jimmy and Billy were adamant she wasn't and, with no other evidence to prove she was, we had no other choice, other than to arrest Jimmy."

"And the Riley's?"

"Well, Billy initially made a statement stating that he'd seen Jimmy attack Finnegan, but not the actual stabbing then, when news got out about their involvement in setting up a local man, all be it a well-known burglar, there were several incidents which culminated in their caravan being torched after which, they disappeared."

"Did you ever bottom out why her DNA was on the knife."

"Apparently, she'd been butchering a rabbit with it earlier in the day and, left it in their caravan," James Cooke said, before John Griffiths could speak.

"Yes, that's right, and forensics confirmed the presence of rabbit blood on the knife," John Griffiths added.

"So, Billy could have been carrying it on the night?"

"Yes, but as Jimmy and Finnegan had also been in the caravan that day, they couldn't be ruled out either," John Griffiths said, the furrows on his brow deepening, "you see, all three were wearing gloves and, when the Riley's disappeared, Jimmy's defence barrister put forward the suggestion that Finnegan had been carrying the knife, tucked into the waist band of his trousers and, during the fight, it had fallen out and somehow, he stabbed himself in the small of the back."

"Were the emergency services called?"

"No, with Finnegan writhing in pain and screaming, Jimmy panicked and ran off, leaving him to bleed to death, which is why, he eventually received the manslaughter sentence."

"But what about Billy Riley, why wasn't he charged?"

"Apparently, when the fight started he was still lying on the floor, which is why he witnessed the first few punches being thrown, but then, when he saw Finnegan drop to his knees clutching his back, he thought he was next and so, he ran away, leaving Jimmy standing over Finnegan a fact, which Jimmy confirmed in interview."

"Do you think Jimmy Hinchcliffe stabbed Finnegan?"

"I couldn't say one way or another, but Jimmy always maintained that he didn't and, well, with no evidence to confirm or contradict him, we had to go with what we had at the time."

"And now?"

"To be perfectly honest with you, I have no idea what about you James?"

"This is your interview John and, to be quite honest, I think you've said more than enough," Chief Superintendent Cook replied, his displeasure and unease, all too apparent.

Chapter 16.

Having gained nothing from the interview, other than a sense of honesty, on the part of Superintendent Griffiths and, serious doubts about the integrity of Chief Superintendent Cooke, Czerniak tasked Danny with checking the CCTV which covered the promenade area of Pensarn on the night of the murders.

Those feelings were further strengthened when, less than twenty minutes later, Danny brought Czerniak, CCTV stills, of John Griffiths, standing on the shoreline and, of the young couple who, had unwittingly, disturbed his suicide attempt.

"Well, that knocks that theory on the head," Czerniak said, as he thumbed through the photographs, "by the way, has Rajni surfaced yet?"

"Yeh, got back about half an hour ago, but since then, she's been interviewing the Iman from the Llandudno mosque.

"The Iman, what the hell has he got to do with this lot?"

"No idea boss, but you know Rajni, when she smells blood."

"Yeh, well it better be worth it, because yet again, she's been missing nearly all bloody day."

When Rajni eventually emerged from the interview room, some hour and a half later, Danny and Tony had already left for the hotel.

"So, are you going to explain, what the hell you've been up to all day and, why you've dragged the bloody Iman in here," Czerniak asked her, as she flopped into a chair.

"Bloody hell boss, give us a few minutes, I'm knackered," she replied, getting up to walk towards their mini kitchen area, "do you want a coffee or something, I'm bloody parched."

"I'll have a black tea and," he started to say.

"Not too strong," she interrupted.

"So, go on, enlighten me," he said as he took the mug of tea from Rajni, "what the hell have you been up to for the last couple of days, while the rest of us have been working this murder case?"

"Hmm, very funny," she replied with a wry smile before taking a sip of her coffee, "god. I needed that, anyway, I don't know if you're going to like this, but I think, I've opened one hell of a large can of worms and, god only knows where it's going to take us."

Over the next half hour and, another two cups of coffee, Rajni explained how she had gone to see Garry Sunderland's ex-wife who, had revealed, a different side, to the womanising used car dealer, they all thought, they knew.

"Yvonne Sunderland, was working as an estate agent when they first met and, actually showed him around the house where he was murdered," Rajni said, whilst continually slaking her thirst with coffee, "she said, he was charming and, a little bit of a flirt, which she said she enjoyed at the time, as her relationship with her then boyfriend was going through a rough patch."

"Does that play any part in this enquiry?" Czerniak asked, "I mean, we already knew they were married, had a child and then divorced."

"Yes, but did you know the child wasn't his?"

"Sorry, what do you mean, wasn't his?"

"The reason her relationship with her previous partner was on shaky ground was, because he'd just learnt about the baby and, didn't believe it was his."

"Christ, what a mess."

"Yes, like you say, a mess, which was only going to get more complicated, when Garry Sunderland did, what he seems to have spent his entire life doing, he used her, to get what he wanted, which in this case, was a mortgage on that property."

"How?"

"By telling her that his finances were in a mess, after a previous business partner, a Mr Cartulary, had defrauded him and numerous customers and, until the case went through the courts, his assets were being frozen."

"And she believed him?"

"Yes, and not only believed him, but took out a mortgage on the property in their joint names, as though they were married."

"I'm sorry, are you saying, they committed mortgage fraud."

"Yep, something which he held over her and, would bring up whenever she questioned his movements."

"Bloody hell Rajni, where is this going, I mean, we know he was a womaniser, so, is she saying he had a string of other women on the hook?"

"No, not exactly, but let's not get ahead of the story," she said with a wry smile, "you see, initially, she thought that his reluctance in the erm, the bedroom department, was due to her size, you know, as she was six months pregnant but, after the baby was born and his attitude towards her continued, she began to suspect he was seeing someone else."

"I take it, she followed him," Czerniak said.

"Oh yes, to a nightclub, but to her surprise, he left it, later that night, arm in arm with some guy."

"Christ, are you saying he was seeing another man?"

"Yes, and one in particular, Baris Dogan."

"Are you sure about all of this, I mean, a woman scorned and all that?"

"That's what I initially thought and so, I pressed her and she assured me, that despite following her husband for many weeks, she only ever saw him with Baris Dogan," Rajni said, as she made another cup of coffee, "now then, she knew that Dogan was gay and so, began to question her own relationship with Garry, you know, from the point of view, that their sex life was non-existent."

"This is getting rather deep isn't it?"

"Yes, however, when she did start to think more about their sex life or, lack of it and, his endless stream of lies and the fact, that he seemed to be spending a great deal of time with Baris Dogan, she decided to confront him."

"Is that what led to their divorce?"

"That, and the fact, that after she'd questioned Garry about his relationship with Dogan, our on-line businessman threatened her."

"Threatened her, how?"

"Apparently, unknown to her and, using another name, Dogan made an appointment with her office, to view an isolated cottage out in the sticks and, when she got there, he arrived and threatened to slit her throat if she ever told anyone about his relationship with Garry."

"Bloody hell, it certainly paints Dogan in a different light, but are we sure, I mean, I know he's a bit of a recluse but, is he gay."

"Well, all the initial outward indications were, that he and Cartulary were players and would chase anything in a skirt but, my little chat with the Iman revealed that it might all have been a façade, you see, under Islamic law, homosexuality is forbidden but, as the Iman said, he is living in a Western world where such things are accepted and therefore, he has at times, turned a blind eye to such activities."

"So, are you saying, the Iman knew Cartulary was gay?"

"Yes, and because they didn't flaunt their relationship, he did nothing to discourage it, in fact, he had used their bank to send money to a family friend."

"Hmm, you say that Dogan threatened to slit Mrs Sunderland's throat, did she believe it was a credible threat?"

"Apparently, he told her he'd already dug a grave for her in the garden of the property and, after he'd gone, she found a freshly dug hole."

"Christ, pretty convincing then?"

"Yes, especially as he said he would also kill her daughter, which is the reason, she quickly upped sticks and moved to Chester, oh, and one other thing, it seems that Dogan was none too pleased when Sunderland, moved Mrs Griffiths into his property."

"Good work Rajni, yeh, bloody good job, now let's get to that bloody hotel, I'm starving."

Over diner that evening, Czerniak and Rajni brought Danny and Tony up to speed after which, the team were told, to spend the following day, verifying, every single detail Baris Dogan had previously provided.

It was mid-morning, when Danny finally heard back from Garry Sunderland's mortgage provider, who confirmed, that the property in Forydd Road, was still under joint names and, as far as they were aware, neither of the co-owners had applied for a loan, against the value of the property.

More or less, the same information came back from Garry Sunderland's bank, who stated, that whilst his finances weren't, what they might consider to be constantly buoyant, he was none the less, in the black at the time of his death and, other than his prearranged overdraft of two thousand pounds, he had no other form of loan agreement with them.

The team, had also spent time, painstakingly trawling through the documents relating to the Hawala Bank, which had been found in the car showroom safe.

With everything pointing to the fact, that Dogan and Cartulary, had initially run the bank jointly, the team failed to find any irregularities or, as they had previously been led to believe, that monies had been misappropriated.

"All this talk of running up debts with the Turkish Mafia, is a load of shite," Tony said, as he threw a thick ledger onto his desktop, "because, from what I can see here, it's just a bunch of out of date old men, using a banking system that went out with ark."

"Yes, I agree," Czerniak replied as he looked up from the pile of documents he was reading, "I mean, in an age when you can safely transfer thousands of pounds to anywhere in the world, why would anyone trust, of all people, a used car dealer, in a back-street garage, to send their hard-earned cash abroad, it just doesn't make sense."

"So, are we going to lift Dogan?" Tony asked.

"Well, he's certainly got some questions to answer because, from what we've found out so far, he's been lying through his bloody teeth from day one."

For the rest of that day, they gathered together all the data they had on the Hawala bank and anything else, which proved that Baris Dogan was more involved in the case than he had originally claimed.

With their arrest and interview package prepared, a search warrant obtained and, a scenes of crime search team briefed, ready for an early morning raid on Dogan's house, the team headed back to their hotel.

The five o'clock alarm was, both shrill and sharp and, cursing the fact, that he'd spent longer than intended the previous night, re-reading the old medical files, Czerniak dragged himself out of bed, whilst at the same time, trying to smother his mobile phone with a pillow.

After a quick shower and, a mouthful of lukewarm instant coffee, which he spat out in disgust, Czerniak hurried downstairs and, was pleased to see that he wasn't the last team member to arrive.

"Where's Danny?" he asked Tony, who was yawning loudly.

"On his way," he replied between yawns, "think he had to dash back to the bog, I told him last night, that the curry was a bad idea."

As they exited the hotel, the heavily, leaden sky loomed low above their heads and, on reaching their cars, a clap of thunder and a flash of lightening, warned all four, of the approaching storm.

Even before Czerniak managed to negotiate the narrow, hotel carpark entrance, the torrential rain, had started to turn the roadway into a river.

Grateful, that he'd briefed the SOCO search team the previous night, he telephoned John Owen, their team leader and told him, to make for the rendezvous point.

With the heavy and persistent rain, making visibility difficult, Czerniak, who was driving the lead vehicle, steered onto the petrol station forecourt and flashed his headlights at John Owen's people carrier.

Chapter 17.

At precisely, 6.15am, the teams two cars, following closely behind the people carrier, containing the SOCO search team, arrived at the narrow entrance, to the windswept cul-de-sac, containing Dogan's house.

It was, at this point, that Czerniak's meticulously planned operation began to go wrong, as no one, in their wildest dreams, could have envisaged, that one of Dogan's neighbours would have chosen that day, of all days, to move house.

The large removal van, was parked, half on and half off the pavement and, as it was partially blocking the entrance to the cul-de-sac, the people carrier couldn't progress any further.

In order to attract the attention of the driver of the removal van, who appeared to be asleep in the cab, the officer in charge of the SOCO people carrier, without thinking of the consequences, sounded the vehicles horn several times.

The driver of the removal van however, was either in a very deep sleep or, just reluctant to move his vehicle and, as such, it remained there blocking the police convoy.

Knowing that the element of surprise was all important and, ignoring the torrential rain, Czerniak leapt from his car and, having hammered on the side door of the people carrier, he yelled for everyone to move.

Now on foot and, already soaked to the skin, the team rushed towards the house and, once he'd received notification, that the rear of the house was secure, Czerniak gave the order to force an entry through the front door.

Knowing, that the property was split level and, that the bedrooms were mostly on the ground floor, the search teams charged forward.

However, having heard the call, of "clear", coming from the teams searching the three downstairs bedrooms, Czerniak and Tony raced upstairs.

The bed, in the large and spacious upstairs bedroom was made and, as it was obviously empty, they dashed from there, into the adjacent lounge/diner.

Slumped on one of the large, red leather sofas, Baris Dogan was mumbling incoherently and, it was only when Tony switched on the lights in the room, that they saw his blood-soaked shirt.

With any thoughts of making an arrest, now completely gone from his mind, Czerniak rushed forward, to try and find the source of the blood.

Ripping open Dogan's shirt, Czerniak immediately saw he had an injury high on his left shoulder.

"Christ almighty," he yelled, as he pressed his hand over the small round hole, "I think he's been shot, quick, get an ambulance."

With the house, now a potential crime scene, all doors and windows were checked, as the search team looked for a point of entry and, to ensure, that the offenders, were no longer in the premises.

"Who did this Baris, who shot you?" Czerniak asked several times, but the young man was already unconscious and therefore, made no reply.

With Tony, accompanying him in the ambulance, Dogan was rushed to the nearest hospital, leaving Czerniak with a dilemma.

Should he continue with his search of the house, to try to find evidence, linking Dogan with the first two murders or, should he and his team vacate the premises and leave it to the local C.I.D to investigate this shooting.

In fact, when Chief Superintendent Cooke arrived, accompanied by the head of C.I.D Detective Chief Superintendent Wilkins and his aide, Detective Chief Inspector Chandler, the decision was very quickly taken out of his hands.

"Thank you, Inspector, we will take it from here," DCS Wilkins said, in a very terse manner, "and, I would be grateful, if your statements were submitted to me by the end of the day."

"But, with all due respect sir, surely you can see that this hinges on the double murder we're investigating," Czerniak argued.

"You heard what DCS Wilkins had to say on the matter," Chief Superintendent Cooke said, as he stepped directly between Czerniak and the senior detective, "now then, can I suggest you return to St Asaph and carry out your duties, as per his instructions."

As he returned to his car, Czerniak's anger was all too apparent and, after practically ripping off his white, forensic suit he slammed the boot lid, got into the vehicle and yelled, at the top of his voice.

"What's the matter with these people, Christ all bloody mighty, are they bloody blind as well as stupid?"

"You're fighting a losing battle boss and you know it," Rajni said, trying her best to calm Czerniak down, "like you said at the outset, they don't want us here and, brining in the top brass like that, tells me, they certainly don't want us treading on their toes, in what they see as a domestic shooting."

"Yeh, come to think of it, it was a bit top heavy, I mean, when was the last time you saw the head of C.I.D attend the scene of a crime?"

"To be honest with you, I don't even know who ours is," she said with a slight giggle, happy that Czerniak had calmed down.

"Right, get hold of Tony and tell him to hang on at the hospital until he's physically removed, because if Dogan wakes up, I want to know, chapter and bloody verse, about who shot him and, before that lot, can change the narrative."

As per the direct orders from DCS Wilkins, Czerniak, Rajni and Danny all wrote a duty statement, detailing why they were at Dogan's house that morning and, the part each of them played.

Meanwhile, due to a misunderstanding in the communications department, Tony remained the only detective standing next to Dogan's hospital bed, but for how long, was anyone's guess.

In fact, it was nearly midday, before DCI Chandler, who was heading up the enquiry, realised that DS Tony Smith, was not one of his own officers and, another thirty minutes, before he got some local detectives to attend.

"Jesus Christ, anyone who saw them bundling me out of that hospital, would have thought I was some sort of criminal," Tony said, as he returned to the incident room.

"Did they actually manhandle you?" Rajni asked.

"As good as, and believe me, if I meet that D/S again in a dark alley, then he's in for."

"Yeh, that'll do Tony," Czerniak said quickly, as he saw D/S Jarvis, their liaison officer entering the room.

"Seems you lot have ruffled a few feathers this morning," D/S Jarvis said with a smirk, as he popped a mint into his mouth.

"Just as well, that you weren't there then," Tony replied sarcastically, "as god only knows what it would have done for your future prospects."

"I beg your pardon," D/S Jarvis said angrily.

"Okay, okay, calm down," Czerniak yelled, "look we're all a bit tense today, so, perhaps you'll cut my team a little slack."

"Hmm, you won't be hearing the last of this," Jarvis said, as he stormed out of the office.

"Ooh, now whose feathers have been ruffled," Tony quipped, as the door slammed shut behind D/S Jarvis.

"That'll do Tony," Czerniak said quietly, "listen, you need to be careful around people like him, as they've always got a friend in high places who can cause you grief."

"Yeh, I know boss, but the man is an absolute arse."

"That's maybe, but we need to keep him on side, especially as we're running out of friendly faces down here."

"Do you really think they'd move us back to London, before we've solved the case?" Rajni asked.

"I think our Chief Superintendent Cooke, would like nothing better," Czerniak replied, "because I've got a sneaky feeling, there's a lot of things hidden within this force, which he in particular, doesn't want seeing the light of day."

"Oh, by the way boss, after they stitched him up, Dogan came around for a short while in the hospital," Tony said, as he casually strolled over to the tea making facilities.

"Jesus Christ, and, come on, what did he have to say?" Czerniak asked urgently, anxious to hear the news before D/S Jarvis returned.

"Well, he was just mumbling at first, you know, as you would expect of someone coming out of sedation."

"Yes, yes, but what did he say about the shooter?"

"Well, apparently, having ordered a pizza, he opened his front door at around 9.30pm last night and, instead of a Dominos scooter outside, there was a man in a ski mask."

"Hang on a minute, is he saying he was shot at 9.30 last night, because if he is, he's lying as that bullet wound was still bleeding," Czerniak said abruptly.

"Yeh, your right it was, but from what he says, it didn't happen until much later," Tony replied, "as he reckons, he was dragged upstairs by the guy and, questioned at gunpoint, about where he stashed his valuables."

"Did he say what valuables?"

"Money, money and jewellery, or so he thought."

"Did they get any?"

"Well, he reckons the guy dragged him back downstairs to his garage, where he thinks he got a couple of thousand in cash, plus an assortment of very valuable watches, possibly worth about the same again."

"So, why shoot him then?"

"Oh, yeh, well, he says that at one stage, the guy got angry over some records or something and, after dragging him upstairs started to threaten him with the gun."

"Angry over what records?" Czerniak asked, a little perplexed

"Yeh, he wasn't making much sense to me at this time, but what he did say, was when this guy kept prodding him with the gun and asking him where everything else was, he just lost it and tried to overpower the fella."

"And what, got shot for his troubles."

"Apparently, it was all over very quickly, he says he got up to lunge at the guy and, as he got hold of him, the gun went off."

"Did he have any idea who he was?"

"Yeh, well I did ask him if he thought it was linked to Cartulary," Tony replied, before taking a sip of his tea, "but, he was, how shall I put it, a little evasive."

"In what way?"

"Well, I asked about accents and of course if his attacker could have been Turkish?"

"Subtle as ever," Danny said with a slight chuckle.

"Yeh, well, you know, with him previously suggesting that money, belonging to this Turkish gangster had gone missing from their bank, I thought I would dangle a worm in front of his face to see if he would bite."

"And, did he?"

"No, which surprised me," Tony replied, before taking another gulp of tea, "in fact, he thought the guy, might have been local, with a slight Liverpool twang."

"Christ, what the hell does that mean?" Danny asked.

"Apparently, it's quite common in and around the Rhyl area and, because of the influx of Liverpudlians into the region, a high proportion of people, now speak with a scouse accent."

"What, and Dogan told you all that?" Danny asked in disbelief.

"No, Glyn, the male nurse treating him, because he reckons, that over half the population of Rhyl are originally from Liverpool."

"So, was anything said, that would make him think it was linked to our job?"

"Erm, just that he felt the guy, knew about the Hawala bank, because he kept asking where Dogan kept the records."

"Records?"

"Yeh, records or recordings and he assumed, he meant of the Hawala transactions."

"Any idea how long he was in the house?"

"Not exactly, because Dogan passed out after being shot, but he seems to think it was well after midnight before the guy left."

"Just one thing," Rajni asked, "why didn't he phone for help, I mean, he could have died from loss of blood."

"Yeh, I asked him that, but he just shrugged and said he didn't know."

"Odd," Czerniak said, scratching his head, "but good work Tony."

Chapter 18.

"So, where do we go from here boss?" Rajni asked, as they sat in the incident room, eating the sandwiches, they'd purchased from a local bakery.

"Good question Rajni," Czerniak replied, "and to be perfectly honest, I have no idea, because our main contender, for suspect number one, is in hospital having been shot and, as it's quite possible, it was for the same reason as his partner, it begs the question, are we barking up the wrong tree, and if so, what have we missed."

"listen, and don't get me wrong, because I think Dogan is as slippery and as bigger liar as his bloody partner," Tony said quietly, "but what if and, it is a bloody big if, he's right and it is locals, I mean, wasn't there a couple of similar jobs on the Cheshire border."

"Yes, you're right Tony, there were and so, how about you liaise with D/I Bob Knight over in

Flint and see there are any similarities with the jobs."

For the next two days, the team kept their heads down, mostly to avoid the wrath of the Welsh police senior management, but also, after a phone call from a very agitated DCI Andrews, back in London, who had told Czerniak, in very plain terms, that following a complaint from Chief Superintendent Cooke, their position, was being closely monitored by the Home Office.

Then, just as Czerniak was about to head out for a meeting with D/I Knight in Flint, he received a phone call from DCI Chandler.

"Erm, Chandler here," the DCI said rather awkwardly over the phone, "listen, there has been a development, which I feel duty bound to share with you."

"A development sir?" Czerniak asked, curious as to why the DCI wanted to share some information with him of all people.

"Yes, erm, forensics have examined the bullet removed from Mr Dogan's sofa," he said, again sounding rather awkward, "and, well, there is no easy way for me to say this, but it looks like it's from the same gun that killed your two victims."

"So, what are you saying sir?"

"Christ almighty Inspector, do I have to spell it out for you," he replied angrily, "the Dogan case is now part of your enquiry and as such, I'm having all the documents sent over to you."

"And the exhibits sir?" Czerniak asked quite bluntly, "when will I have access to them?"

"Exhibits?"

"Well, I take it, your team will have done a full forensic sweep of the house."

"I'm sorry, that's something you'll need to bring up with D/S Dan Davis, as after I left the scene, to brief the team and set up an incident room, he was the man on the ground so to speak, now then, if there's nothing else, I'll bid you good day," he replied before putting the phone down and ending their conversation.

A quick phone call with DS Davis soon revealed, that due to the lack SOC officers, only a very basic forensic search had been carried out at the address and, except for a few photographs and the bullet, which had been dug out of the wooden framework of the sofa, there was nothing.

After swearing loudly and, throwing a telephone directory across the room, Czerniak tried to calm down, before making a call to John Owen, head of the Wales SOCO team.

"Why wasn't that bloody house searched from top to bottom?" Czerniak demanded angrily, unable to contain his frustration.

"Because, like you, we were ordered out of there."

"By who, for Christ's sake?" he asked, now a little calmer.

"Chief Superintendent Cooke."

"Did he say why?"

"Something about cross contamination, because Brian, who was part of my team, had searched Sunderland Motors."

"But that's ridiculous, I mean, if that was the case, why not just ask him to leave?"

"That's what I said, but he was insistent and so, as he was the senior officer at the scene, we had no other choice, but to leave."

"Do you know if he called in another team to search?"

"Well, if he did, it would have been from out of the force area, because I know none of my lads went back there."

"Hmm, can you put together a team and meet me there in an hour, we need to go over the place, with the old, fine tooth comb."

With Tony and Rajni now dispatched to Flint to keep his appointment with DI Knight, Czerniak and Danny headed over to the home of Baris Dogan.

Anxious, not to compromise the scene any more than it had been already, Czerniak and Danny waited outside the premises and, only entered, when John Owen finally gave them the all clear.

"Anything of any significance?" Czerniak asked, as he stepped in through the front door.

"Well, we've lifted a number of prints, from the strongbox, where the money and jewellery were allegedly stored, but we won't know if they belong to the victim or the offenders or, even senior police officers, until I run them through the system."

"Jesus Christ, you don't mean, they waltzed about the house without gloves?"

"Seems, that some people haven't heard of DNA yet," he replied with a smirk.

"Or fingerprints by the sound of it, Christ, are they bloody dinosaurs or what?"

"Arrogant, is probably a better description."

"Did you find anything else?"

"Nothing of any great value, except to say, that judging by the spray pattern of the blood and the fact that the bullet was found lodged in the wooden framework, your victim was shot on, or close to the settee where he was found."

"So, he wasn't standing up?"

"Is that what he says?"

"Well yes, as he reckons, he'd lunged at the man with a gun and it had gone off in the struggle."

"Hmm, well if I was to hazard a guess, only because of the location of the bullet hole in the settee, I'd say he was sitting down," he replied, pointing towards the circular tear in the red leather, "but there again, the pattern could well be similar, if he was, let's say, stumbling backwards towards the settee, look, I'm no expert in blood spray analysis, so maybe give the forensic lab in Chorley a ring and ask for Dianne Shaw."

Once John Owen and his team had left the premises, Danny and Czerniak began a search of their own, only this time, they were looking for evidence, to link Dogan, to the murders of Garry Sunderland and Linda Griffiths.

They commenced their search, in the integral garage, from where Dogan ran his jewellery business and, Czerniak was immediately struck by how tidy everything seemed.

"Erm, is it me, I mean, from my point of view, someone, desperately searching for money and jewellery, would have ransacked this place."

"Yes, unless of course he struck lucky and found the strongbox straight away," Danny replied, pointing towards the heavy metal box, which was bolted to the brick wall, "I mean, it is quite obvious."

"Hmm, yeh, I suppose you're right, but all the same, I'd have expected more of a mess."

"I tell you what is strange though," Danny said, as he examined the strong box more closely, "this was opened with a key and not forced."

"Did Tony ask him about that?"

"Shall I give him a bell?"

"Yes and, while you're at it, ask him if Dogan said anything about being questioned about the money."

Whilst Danny made the phone call, Czerniak started going through the drawers, of the only desk in the room and soon, came across a series of letters from creditors, some of whom were threatening legal action, if Dogan didn't settle his debts.

"Tony reckons, the guy roughed Dogan up a bit and asked him about the money, but no mention was made of a key or how quickly they found it," Danny said, after finishing his phone call.

"That's very convenient, especially when you see, just how much, our so called, successful business man was in debt," Czerniak replied, as he handed Danny some of the creditor's letters.

"Christ, how much does he owe?"

"After a quick look at this lot, I'd say about ten maybe twelve grand and the question is, if you've got a couple of thousand stashed away in your strongbox, why not pay some of them off."

"So, do you think he's lying about the robbery?"

"Yes, trouble is, that bullet hole in his shoulder is real."

For the next couple of hours, the two men continued searching the large, detached house, ending up, at 6.45pm in the kitchen.

"To be honest with you Dan, I'm knackered and, as I can't see any value in going over where we've already searched, can I ask you to photograph each room before we go."

Whilst Danny took the photographs, Czerniak stood and stared at the red leather settee where he'd discovered Dogan and, tried to gage if the victim could have been falling backwards as he claimed, when he was shot.

Then, using the end of a pencil, pushed into the bullet hole, he tried to work out the angle of trajectory."

"Any joy?" Danny asked, when he saw Czerniak bent double over the settee.

"No, trouble is the hole has been enlarged, by whoever dug the bullet out, so there's no way of saying for certain, where he was when the gun was fired."

"Maybe that blood spatter expert could help."

"Yes, let's get her here first thing tomorrow."

Then, with Danny, arranging over the telephone, for Dianne Shaw to attend the scene the following morning, Czerniak drove them back to St Asaph.

"How did you two get on in Flint," Czerniak asked Tony and Rajni as he walked into the incident room.

"Not very well I'm afraid," Tony replied, "because for one thing, the gun their witness described, was far too small to be a nine millimetre, which is what forensics are saying our shooter used."

"Any other bad news?"

"Yeh, Bob Knight is convinced that his job was down to some local idiot."

"Why do you say it like that?"

"Because, intelligence is coming in, that some numpty, a lad called Garry Car, has suddenly come into a bit of money," he replied, "and, instead of keeping his head down, he's just bought himself a BMW."

"You are joking?"

"No, you couldn't make it up," he said, handing a copy of the intel sheet to Czerniak, "and, two days after the job, he was booking a flight to Malaga for him and his misses."

"Has he been lifted?"

"Not yet, because he's still enjoying his all-inclusive holiday in the Hotel Splendid."

"Is he going to extradite him?"

"No, he's back on Friday, so he'll be arrested as he steps off the plane."

"So, there's no way he's in the frame for shooting Dogan?"

"No, not unless he popped back for the night."

"Shit!"

Chapter 19.

The following morning, whilst Rajni, accompanied Danny and Dianne Shaw to the crime scene, Czerniak and Tony went the hospital in Bodelwyddan, to record a formal statement from Baris Dogan.

Claiming to still be in some pain, Dogan initially refused to speak with them however, when Czerniak mentioned the fact, that unless he cooperated, they would be forced to contact his bank, for details of the stolen money, he reluctantly agreed to make a brief statement.

After allowing Dogan, to tell them a very brief synopsis of the events that night, Czerniak began to probe and ask for more detail.

"How tall would you say, the man with the gun was?" was he his opening question.

"Oh, erm slightly taller than me, maybe six foot," he replied with some confidence.

"And build?"

"Erm, stocky, yes stocky, but it's quite difficult to say for sure, because he was wearing one of those puffer jackets."

"Yes, I see what you mean, they could quite easily give you the wrong impression," Czerniak said, as though he was agreeing with Dogan.

"Yes," Dogan replied very quickly.

"But, there again, when you grappled with him, you'd have got a better idea of how big he was."

"Erm, yes, I mean no, you see, it was all so quick because, as soon as he saw me getting up, he pushed me back and shot me."

"Oh, I see, so, you didn't actually get hold of him?"

"No, I had only just managed to get to my feet so, I suppose I was a little off balance."

"Yes, I can see how that would happen, but the sound of the gun going off, surely it should have alerted one of your neighbours."

"Well no, what I mean is, I think it was fitted with a silencer, because there was only a loud pop, which is why, I didn't know I'd been shot at first."

"Didn't you feel the pain?"

"Yes, but I thought it was from him punching me or something, it was only when I rubbed my shoulder that I saw the blood and, I think I must have passed out."

"And you've no idea how long you were unconscious?"

"Erm, it's difficult to say, because I think I came around once or twice and then, when I tried to move, I passed out again."

"It must have been extremely painful," Czerniak said, trying to sound sympathetic, "have the doctors giving you any idea if there is going to be any lasting damage?"

"Erm, apparently, the bullet only scraped the top of my left clavicle so, they're hopeful of a full recovery."

"Bloody hell, that was a stroke of luck, I mean, a fraction lower and you may have lost the use of your arm."

"Yes, as you say, I have to be grateful for small mercies," he replied with a weak smile.

"So, whilst we're on the subject of the gun, have you any idea what sort of weapon it was?"

"Erm, I'm afraid I know very little about firearms, except to say, it was obviously a handgun."

"What about colour and shape?"
"Black or dark blue and sort of square."
"And the silencer?"
"Same I think."
"My colleague here, tells me the man who shot you was asking about some records, what records would they be?"
"Records or recordings, I don't really remember," he replied with a vague look on his face, "anyway, what so important about that?"
"Sorry, but every aspect about this important."
"Yes, that's what the other police officer said."
"Which one?"
"Oh, I don't know, bit older than you, but in uniform."
"Hmm, oh yes," Czerniak suddenly said, pretending to have just remembered something else, "your strongbox was opened with the key, how did he know where to find it?"
"Erm, yes, the key, well, it was, it was around my neck on a chain, a gold chain which I think he also took," he replied nervously.
"Was it visible?"
"What the chain?"

"No Mr Dogan, the key, would it have been visible, would they have seen it hanging from the chain around your neck?"

"Well, it must have been, otherwise, how would he have known about it?"

"Do you always carry the key on your chain?"

"Erm, as a rule yes."

"And, would it have been common knowledge amongst your friends, that you carried the key to your strongbox around your neck?"

"Did I advertise it do you mean, then if so, the answer is a very definite no, but one or two of my closest confidants would have known."

"Including Georgio Cartulary?"

"Erm, yes, he would have known, but why do you ask about him, I mean, Georgio couldn't have had anything to do with this, because he's dead isn't he?"

"Yes, I'm afraid he is, but, I'm just exploring all avenues at the moment and, as you were both shot, I can't rule out the fact that both incidents are linked."

"But I thought that Georgio and that woman were killed by the Turkish Mafia," he suddenly blurted out.

"That's one theory yes," Czerniak replied, a little taken aback by Dogan's outburst, "but we are currently pursuing many other lines of enquiry."

"Can I ask what they are?" He demanded, now sitting upright in his hospital bed.

"I'm afraid, because of operational matters, I am not at liberty to divulge those details at this present time," Czerniak replied, with a rather stern, fixed stare, he hoped would calm Dogan down and, help him to focus on the facts, "now then, can you tell me, the origins of the money, you say was stolen."

For the next twenty minutes, Dogan ducked and dodged around the question of the money and, with no real answer as to where it had come from or, if it existed at all, Czerniak moved on to the watches which were also, allegedly stolen.

Again, unable to furnish them with a name of his supplier or where they might find details of the watches, Dogan failed to convince Czerniak they had been in the strongbox or, that they had even been stolen.

"So, what you're saying, is that you had five watches in your strongbox, worth a combined total of several thousand pounds and, you have no documentation to show where they came from or, how they came to be in your possession in the first place."

"Look, what you must understand, is that in my line of work, you don't ask too many questions when you are offered a bargain."

"So, are you now saying, that you think the watches might have been stolen property when you purchased them," Czerniak asked, as he leant forward over Dogan's bed.

"Erm, look," he replied quickly and, with a nervous twitch of his left cheek, "I erm, I bought them from one of those online auction sites."

"eBay?"

"Erm, it might have been yes," Dogan replied, as he grabbed the thin duvet and pulled it up to his chest, "trouble is, I trawl all sorts of sites like that, literally from all over the world, so they could have come from almost anywhere, look, I wish I could help you more, but I'm feeling very tired right now and, to be quite honest with you, I would like you both to leave."

With his nurse, insisting that he be left in peace, Czerniak and Tony had very little choice but to leave the ward.

As they walked out of the hospitals main entrance, Czerniak switched his mobile phone back on and contacted Rajni.

"How did you get on at Dogan's place," he asked, whilst trying to get out the way of a speeding ambulance.

"We're still there," she replied.

"Why, is there a problem?"

"Erm, it's Danny, he's got it into his brain that there's something odd about one of the walls in the lounge and, to be quite honest with you, he's doing my head in," she replied, the tiredness and frustration, only too apparent in her voice.

"Why, what's wrong with it?" Czerniak demanded, his voice raised over the sound of another speeding ambulance.

"He reckons, that it's thicker than it should be or something," she replied, now sounding more annoyed than frustrated, "but, I've looked at it and, so did Dianne Shaw, before she left and, neither of us could see what he's going on about, god only knows what she thought, coz I caught her giggling to herself as she went downstairs."

"What's he doing now?" Czerniak asked, as he got into his vehicle.

"Walking backwards and forwards, taping the wall, like some bloody doctor."

"Okay, I'll be there in about twenty minutes, just give him a cup of tea or something and get him to sit down somewhere."

"What, in a bloody darkened room with cucumbers over his eyes?" she asked, sounding relieved that help was on its way.

"Yeh, something like that,"

As they drove towards Colwyn Bay and the small cul-de-sac where Dogan lived, Czerniak, believing that Danny was having some sort of psychotic episode, began to berate himself for pushing his team so hard.

However, when he and Tony entered the house, they were surprised to find him, both calm and, very lucid.

"So, talk me through it, why do you think this bloody wall is so odd," Czerniak asked, as he stepped into the lounge.

"Well, for one thing, it's wider here," he said, pointing towards the corner of the lounge wall, where it turned into the dining area, "compared to here, in the dining room, do you see what I mean."

Having slowly eyed up the wall in question from the lounge Czerniak, then went into the dining section of the room and, did the same from there.

"Yes, I see it," he said, whilst bent over, running his hand along the wall, "but, it could be something as simple, as the wall in the lounge area being a supporting wall and this one isn't."

"I thought of that to begin with, but, if you come into the kitchen, you can see where the floor units are slightly wider along this first section of wall and, narrower towards the far end," he replied, whilst pointing towards the thinner cupboards.

"Bit odd, but it's probably just a design thing, you know, to get around some structural problem on the inside of the wall."

"Well no, that's just it, you see, if you go downstairs, there is absolutely nothing structural underneath, so I reckon, Dogan has had some sort of stash built into the lounge wall," he said going back into the lounge, "because, if you tap the wall here, it sounds hollow."

Having tapped the wall, several times himself, Czerniak had to agree, that he could hear a slight echo.

"Have you looked for a door or hatch, or some other way of getting behind the wall?" Czerniak asked, as he stepped back to look at the section of wall again.

"Yes, but there's absolutely bugger all, well, from what I can see anyway, which makes it so bloody frustrating," Danny replied

Whilst he stood, staring at the white painted wall, Czerniak's eyes were drawn to a small water colour, depicting a sailboat, struggling in rough seas, which was positioned, just to the right of the hollow section.

"Have you looked behind that painting?" he asked.

"What, oh yes, you can't see behind it, because he's stuck it to the bloody wall for some reason."

"He's done what?"

"Stuck it on the wall, yeh, have a look for yourself," he replied, trying to move the painting, "see, it's not on hangers or anything, just glued in place, bloody odd if you ask me."

"Are you sure it's not hiding something?"

"Not that I can see no and, before you ask boss, yes I've run my hand all around it looking for some sort of catch or lever and, there's bugger all there."

"Hang on a minute," Rajni said, picking up a small, remote-control hand set, she'd found stuffed between two cushions, on the red settee, "what's this for, because it's not for his tv."

Then, as she pressed the only button on the remote-control device, there was a slight click from behind the painting.

"I knew it, it's a bloody stash point," Danny yelled with delight, as he pulled the painting away from the wall on its hinges, "look, there's a wad of cash, a phone and, a bloody gun."

"Don't touch it," Czerniak shouted, as Danny went to put his hand into the small recess, "let's get SOCCO back here and, a firearms officer to make it safe."

Chapter 20.

"It's a Lebdev 9-millimetre boss," the firearms officer said, as he handed, the exhibits bag to Czerniak, "made in Russia by our old friend, Mr Kalashnikov or, so I believe."

"And the silencer?"

"Looks to be a professional job," he replied, "but I've got no idea where it was manufactured as there are no markings on it."

"When you say, a professional job, I take it, you mean, that it wasn't knocked together in some back-street garage?"

"Well, if it was, they were very well equipped," he replied, before taking another quick look at the silencer, "and, if you look here, you can see how well it's been finished off, no, if I had to put my money on it, I'd say it was made to fit this particular gun."

"In the Lebdev factory?"

"Yes boss, that would be my best guess."

"So, the question is, was Dogan shot by the so-called intruder or, did he see us coming and shoot himself, to throw us off the scent," Czerniak asked Danny, "because, unless I'm very much mistaken, that stash point was closed when we found him on that settee."

"Yes, it was and, if you're asking for my opinion, I know where my money is going," Danny replied.

"Yeh, me too and, the moment he's fit enough to be moved from his hospital bed, that lying little bastard, is getting locked up," Czerniak snarled.

As they pulled into the car park at St Asaph police station, D/I Mel Jones was sitting in his car and, very obviously waiting for them.

"I need to speak to you urgently," he said, after hurrying over to Czerniak, "but not here."

"Well, I'm about to nip back to our hotel if that's any good for you."

Twenty minutes later and, acting like a pair of highly suspicious characters, Czerniak and D/I Jones, who had arrived in the hotel carpark separately, were now, huddled together, in a corner of the hotels, empty bar.

"Look, there is no easy way to say this, but I think, there's a very good chance that Jimmy Hinchcliffe was murdered," Mel Jones said, whilst nervously looking around the empty room.

"Bloody hell," Czerniak said, hoping this wasn't going to complicate an already complex situation, "are you sure, I mean, I hate to say it, but you were wrong about John Griffiths, so, what makes you so certain that Hinchcliffe was murdered?"

"Because, the pathologist found marks on Jimmy's wrists, which indicate, that he was restrained, possibly by handcuffs, just before he died."

"Shit, how certain is he, I mean, narrowing it down specifically to handcuffs, that's pretty dam conclusive?"

"As certain, as any pathologist, with his experience could be under the circumstances," he replied, "plus the fact, that the heroin in his system, was almost pure."

"Well, that's not good," Czerniak said, before asking who else was aware of the post mortem results.

"No one other than me, though, as he was a registered informant, I suppose at some stage, it will need, to be flagged up to professional standards."

"So, what do you intend doing with the information now?"

"Well, before I do anything, there is one important question I want answering."

"Which is what exactly?"

"Hmm, where do I begin, you see, a few years ago, erm, and not long after Mary died, John and I, well, we used to get very drunk together and, during one of those drunken nights, we erm, started telling each other things, you know, which under normal circumstances, we wouldn't have shared with anyone. Anyway, he told, or should I say, he started to tell me, before thinking better of it, something, about a recorded conversation and how, if it hadn't had been for the recording, Jimmy Hinchcliffe would have gone down for life," he said, now nervously wringing his hands together.

"Yes, he told me something about it, when I interviewed him," Czerniak said, not understanding, what relevance this new information played, "wasn't it, Billy Riley, or if not, his wife who taped Hinchcliffe when he was trying to get some information about a guy called Finnegan?"

"No, no, you don't understand, it was John who made the recording and so, as I've got nothing else to lose, career wise anyway, I'm going to confront him and, sort it out once and for all because, I really believe its's behind everything that's happened."

"Bloody hell, is that wise, I mean, because as things stand right now, it's odds on, that Baris Dogan is our killer, so dragging up the past and upsetting a Superintendent, might not be in your best interest, you know, given as you're already facing some sort of disciplinary hearing."

"Look, it's good of you to think like that, but no, my career, in C.I.D anyway, is over, so, while I still can, I need to resolve this matter and, as he's off duty today, I can speak to him alone in his house and, more importantly, away from prying eyes and ears."

Still not certain, what he should do with this new information and how, if at all, it related to the two murders he was investigating, Czerniak headed back to St Asaph and, the incident room.

"Two interesting bits of news just in boss," Rajni said, as Czerniak walked into the room, "firstly, the phone we found in Dogan's stash, is the pay as you go mobile, that was used to send messages to Gary Sunderland."

"Which, more or less confirms, what Sunderland's ex wife and the Iman said about the two of them being an item," Czerniak replied.

"Exactly what I was thinking, plus, it gives him the oldest motive in the world for murder, a scorned lover," she said, looking quite pleased with herself.

"Agreed, so, what else?"

"Sorry?"

"You said you had two bits of information?"

"Oh yeh, sorry, got a bit carried away, so yeh, it looks like our gun, the one in Dogan's stash, might have been part of a shipment, seized from a Bulgarian tanker off the Welsh coast."

"Christ almighty, when was that?"

"About six months ago, in a place called, hang on a minute, how would you pronounce that," she replied, showing him the word Llandulas.

"Do we know where it is?" he asked.

"Erm, apparently, it's not far from Colwyn Bay, seems there's a local quarry in that place," she replied, avoiding the word, Llandulas, "which uses a jetty or pier thing, jutting out into the sea, to load gravel onto small boats, or should that be ships, anyway, they get filled with stone there."

"Hmm, yes, and the guns?" He asked impatiently.

"Oh, yeh, sorry, erm, seems local special branch, had received a tip off about guns being imported through small docks and the like and, after a search of a Bulgarian registered tanker, erm, called, Gustav V, they found five, Lebdev, nine-millimetre handguns, all with silencers and, five hundred rounds of ammo."

"And, what makes you think our gun was part of that haul?"

"Because, one is now missing, well it was, until it turned up in Dogan's house."

"Our we sure of this?"

"One hundred per cent, as the serial number tallies with one of those seized."

"And, dare I ask, where it was being stored."

"Here, in the basement of this very building," she replied, handing Czerniak, the written proof.

"And the seizing officer, does he play any part in any of this?"

"Oh, erm, D/S Basset, no, well, not that we know of but, the interesting thing is, the seized property register was counter signed by our Superintendent, Mr John Griffiths."

"And, had it been signed out for any reason?"

"No," she replied, looking pensive, "look boss, it's only a thought, but do you think he could have kept one of the guns back because, having been down there in the basement, I would say, it's nigh on impossible to break in and steal anything without being noticed, as for one thing, it's like bloody Fort Knox and another, there's about six cameras in the seized property store."

"Shit," he said suddenly, "Mel Jones has gone to see him alone."

As they ran to the cars, Rajni tried to contact D/I Jones via his mobile phone and, after reaching his answering service for a third time, she called the police control room and asked for an armed response team, to meet them at the home of Superintendent Griffiths.

At that time of day, the ten-mile journey, from St Asaph, to the Abergele home of Superintendent John Griffiths, would normally have taken about fifteen minutes but, by using the cars blue flashing lights and, driving most of the way, on the wrong side of the road, Czerniak made it in just under nine.

With his tyres smoking, as he screeched to a halt outside the address, Czerniak wasn't going to wait for the armed response vehicle to arrive and, ignoring all proper protocols, he kicked the front door open and raced inside.

"What the hell is the meaning of this," John Griffiths yelled, as both he and D/I Mel Jones leapt to their feet.

"Stay exactly where you are," Czerniak yelled back as he raced towards the Superintendent.

Then, before he could say or do anything else, Czerniak knocked the Superintendent to the ground and handcuffed him.

"John Griffiths, I am arresting you on suspicion of murder times two and, the attempted murder of Baris Dogan," then after cautioning him, he dragged John Griffiths, back up onto his feet.

"Have you lost your mind," D/I Jones screamed at Czerniak, "he's innocent, you bloody well told me yourself."

"I've got no time for this right now," Czerniak replied pushing the D/I to one side, so he could walk his prisoner out of the house.

Then, just as he was placing John Griffiths into the rear of his car, the armed response team arrived.

"You need to secure the premises for a forensic search," he yelled at the uniformed officers, as they leapt from their vehicle.

With Rajni driving, they then sped away from the house and, as she headed out of Abergele, John Griffiths spoke for the first time since his arrest.

"Take me to Chester," he demanded, "do you hear, take me to Chester, otherwise you'll never get at the truth."

"But under PACE, I need to take you," Czerniak started to say.

"Yes, yes, to the nearest police station," John Griffiths said interrupting him, "but on this occasion, I think it's better all-round, if I go out of the force area."

Although, sorely tempted to ask John Griffiths, why he was insisting on being taken to a police station, out of his own force area, Czerniak knew this would be deemed as the start of an interview and so, during the half hour journey to Chester, he said, absolutely nothing to his prisoner.

Once he'd been booked in to the custody suite, at Chester's main police station, John Griffiths waved his rights to consult with a solicitor and asked to be interviewed as soon as possible.

"This is highly irregular," Czerniak said, as he and Rajni sat opposite Superintendent Griffiths in the interview room, "so, can you please confirm for the recording device and, those who will listen to it in the future, that you insisted on being brought to this police station in Chester."

"I did," he replied, with a clear voice, "and, to answer your next questions, I have also waved my rights, to consult with a solicitor and, to be interviewed by an officer of equal rank."

"And, you know, that at any time, you can change your mind on either of those points?"

"I do, now, let's get on with it."

"Well, I suppose the obvious place to start would be with your arrest earlier today," Czerniak said, moving awkwardly on his chair, "and to explain, again for the benefit of the recording, that it was on suspicion of murder times two and, attempted murder, can you confirm that please."

"Yes, that's correct and yes, I was then cautioned and given my rights."

"Thank you, now, the murders I spoke of, were, that of Linda Griffiths, your wife and Georgio Cartulary, also known as Garry Sunderland, can you tell me, were you responsible for those murders?"

"No, I was not."

"And the attempted murder, relates to a Baris Dogan, can I ask, are you the person who broke into his home and shot him?"

"No, again, that was not me."

"Can I take you back six months, to a day in late November last year, when D/S Bassett, of the Special Branch, boarded a ship just off the North Wales coast at Llandulas and seized, a number of firearms and ammunition, do you recall the incident?"

"Erm yes, but I played no part in it."

"Were you present, when those firearms were lodged in the seized property room in St Asaph police station?"

"Yes, I believe I was, as D/S Bassett wanted me to oversee the process but, although I was, as you say present, I didn't have any contact with the weapons, as they had to be preserved for forensic examination."

"When did that take place?"

"Erm, to be perfectly honest with you, I have no idea if it ever did because, like I say, I played no part in the seizing of the firearms or the subsequent investigation."

"Are you aware, that a firearm has been recovered from the home of Baris Dogan?"

"Yes, D/I Jones informed me earlier."

"And, would it surprise you to learn, that the firearm in question, was one of those, seized by D/S Bassett in November last year?"

"It was what?" he asked, his face contorted in shock.

"The Lebdev nine-millimetre handgun and silencer, found in Baris Dogan's home, was part of the consignment, seized by D/S Bassett last year, the same firearms, you oversaw being placed in the seized property room at St Asaph police station," Czerniak said, leaning slightly forward over the desk, "did you, take that gun from the seized property room?"

"No, I did not."

"Do you know who did?"

"What, do I think that Jimmy Hinchcliffe broke into the seized property store, stole the gun and gave it to me, so I could shoot my wife and Sunderland?" he replied angrily.

"That's not what I asked, but, as you have brought up his name," Czerniak said, now relaxing back into his seat, "tell me about the recording."

"The recording?" he asked, looking a little uneasy for the first time.

"Yes, the recording, you used, to reduce the charges against Hinchcliffe."

"Erm, well, first of all, what you need to remember, is that Jimmy was my informant and, had been for some time so, I felt I had something of a duty of care towards him."

"Yes, I understand that and would agree with you wholeheartedly, so please, explain what happened, because I believe, what happened back then, played a big part in the events we are investigating."

"Erm, I think it must have been, either my first or second week as a D/I in Abergele and, I was away from the station on an induction course in Headquarters, when my D/S, Graham Salter, received a complaint of rape, from the parents of a schoolgirl, called Emma Watkins," he replied, before pausing for a second. "Of course, with me off the scene, the DCI was called in and that, as you already know, was James Cooke, well, by the time I became involved, he'd already identified Finnegan as the culprit."

"Because of the distinctive tattoo on his neck?"

"Yes, well, that is what I believed at the time."

"Are you saying, that wasn't the case?"

"I'm saying, that I only learnt much later, that the information, about the offender having a tattoo on his neck, well, let's just say, it didn't come from the victim."

"Can I ask, who was the source of that information?"

"In all honesty, I couldn't tell you with any true certainty, but the person who acquired it and then, became the driving force behind it, was DCI Cooke and he, let it be known at the time, that anyone, who disagreed with him, would be down the road."

"Did they have history?"

"Who, Finnegan and James Cooke?"

"Yes, had their paths ever crossed before?" Czerniak asked, knowing how important it was to keep the pressure on the Superintendent.

"The simple answer is, I don't know, but, because he knew so much about him, I very quickly formed the opinion, that at some stage, Finnegan, must have got one over on James and he, of course, was out for revenge."

"Regardless of the outcome?"

"Oh yes, because, as I learnt to my cost, he isn't the type of person you want to cross swords with" he replied with a faint smile, "and so, I very quickly formed the opinion, that he was going to nail Finnegan for the rape and, didn't care one way or the other, if the real offender got off with it."

"So, whose idea was it to use Jimmy Hinchcliffe?"

"Well, after the Riley's gave Finnegan an almost air tight alibi, I have to say, that initially it was mine, you know, because I knew he'd been wheeling and dealing with the other travellers on that site, but my idea was, that Jimmy should play a far subtler role."

"What, go in, ask a few mundane questions about why the Riley's went to the police and admitted stealing lead in Shotton, when in reality, no one had any idea it was them who'd committed the offence and then, when he'd gotten enough, casually leave?"

"Well yes, because let's be fair, we all knew, that the likes of the Riley's, and Finnegan in particular, had lived their entire lives on their wits and, anyone blundering in asking too many questions, would be spotted in a heartbeat."

"But, Chief Superintendent Cooke wasn't happy with that approach?"

"No, and first of all, much to my annoyance, he insisted meeting and then, briefing Jimmy himself."

"How did Jimmy react to that?"

"Not happy, but, when I told him there was a five thousand-pound, Crime Stoppers reward up for grabs, he agreed."

"So, you recorded that meeting?"

"Hmm, very astute," he replied with a faint smile, "yes, I recorded it, using a concealed device."

"And, I take it, that Chief Superintendent Cooke had no idea you were recording him, giving Hinchcliffe his instructions?"

"No, none at all, you see, by that time, I was fully aware, that he was hell bent on fitting up Finnegan for the rape and, well, I was not only watching my back, but Jimmy's as well."

"So, what was on that recording, that was so damming?"

"Erm, well, besides the briefing, there was the conversation, I had with James, immediately after Jimmy Hinchcliffe got out of the car," he replied, his head now slightly bowed, "you see, I'd heard about Finnegan's reputation and, his propensity towards extreme violence and so, I told Cooke, in no uncertain terms, that I thought, he was sending Jimmy on a suicide mission."

"And, what did he say to that?"

"That, if Finnegan killed Jimmy, then it would be a double whammy, because, not only would there be one less junkie on the streets but, he'd also be able to send Finnegan to prison for life."

"Christ Almighty, what did you say to that?"

"I told him, that I was fully aware that Finnegan was not the offender in the rape and, that I wanted no part in setting up an innocent man but, he just ignored me and went on, about how this was a golden opportunity to get a violent man off the streets, to clear up a messy rape case and how, if I wanted to stay on C.I.D, I needed to learn very quickly, that life, was about making those difficult decisions, decisions, which were made, for the better good, of the decent members of the public we served."

"Did you tell him, you'd taped that conversation?"

"Not then no but, when the CPS wanted Jimmy charged with murder, I made him aware of it and the consequences for both of us, if it was ever made public."

"So, he made the Riley's disappear?"

"I always suspected so yes, but had no proof."

"And so, Jimmy faced a lesser charge of manslaughter."

"Yes, but even then, the evidence was week, so he served nine months for breaking and entering and the rest as they say, lay on the file."

"And the recording, where is that now?"

"A good question, you see, I'm afraid those events played very heavily on my mind and, on the rare occasions, when I got very, very drunk, I would apparently say something, which of course was the situation with Mel Jones, though, I only ever told Linda, what was actually on the tape."

"And, did she know where it was kept?"

"Yes, I'm afraid she did and, was using it to force me into making a far larger divorce settlement than she was entitled to."

"She was blackmailing you?"

"Well, that bastard Sunderland, or whatever his real name is, was trying to do so, yes."

"And, who did you tell?"

"Well, as it involved his future as well as my own, I felt, I was duty bound to inform James Cooke."

"And was it him or you, who asked Jimmy Hinchcliffe to break into Sunderland's garage and look for the tape recording."

"I did, or should I say, I was told to ask him."

"And, when did he do that?"

"The night before Linda and Sunderland were shot."

"Did Jimmy find the tape?"

"No, just some cash, which he said, he was keeping, in lieu of payment for the job."

"And, just one last thing for now, why did you go to the hospital, to ask Dogan about the tape recording."

"I didn't."

Chapter 21

"This has never been about anything else, other than, a bent, egotistical, power hungry copper, trying to cover his tracks," Czerniak said, during his, three-way telephone conversation, with DCI Andrews and, George Henson, his Home Office handler, "the question is, how do we prove it because, without that tape recording, we only have the word of John Griffiths, who has already disclosed, that his wife and her lover were blackmailing him, which gives him, a classic motive for murdering both of them."

"Yes, and also, when you take into account, that time wise anyway, his alibi is more than a bit shaky, then it puts him back, firmly in the frame for it," DCI Andrews added

"Plus, we have the anomaly with the gun," George Henson said, "because, have I got this right, wasn't Superintendent Griffiths, one of the last people to have legitimate access to the firearm, used in the two killings and, the attempted murder of Baris Dogan."

"He was, though we have no proof, that he took it," Czerniak replied.

"What about CCTV, in the seized property store?" DCI Andrews asked.

"Yes, it's one of those new computerised systems, with six cameras actually in the room itself but, PC Williams, the officer in charge of the seized property store, tells me, that the bloody thing has been off-line for over a month."

"Please don't tell me, it was Superintendent Griffiths, who was overseeing the problem with the CCTV system," DCI Andrews asked sarcastically.

"Yes, I'm afraid so and, as our PC Williams knew that Superintendent Griffiths was going through a difficult patch, marriage wise, he never pursued the matter with him and why, it's still not working."

"What about the hospital?" George Hanson asked, "have we any idea who it was who visited Dogan and questioned him about the recording?"

"Danny and Tony are heading over to the hospital as we speak, to trawl through their CCTV, so I'll let you know the moment we get a hit."

"What did Dogan have to say about the gun being found in his secret stash?" Andrews asked.

"Well, that's the funny thing, because he claims, he was putting some watches and money into the stash, when his attacker arrived and, as he thought it was just a pizza delivery man, he left it open," Czerniak replied, "however, after being shot, he passed out and, as it was closed when we arrived and he, never actually fully regained consciousness, he's saying, he didn't know it had been searched by the offender or, used to hide the gun."

"So, presumably, he's now saying the gun was planted to implicate him in the killings?" Hanson asked.

"Well, actually, he's not saying anything, as his solicitor has advised him, not to say anything, which, might ultimately endanger his life and as such, he's now refusing to cooperate any further."

"So, what's your next move?" Hanson asked.

"Well, to be perfectly honest with you, as we only have John Griffith's word to go on, I think that ball is very much in your court because, without tangible, irrebuttable proof, I can't see our Chief Superintendent admitting anything, can you?"

"Yes, I agree," Hanson said, "and, as we can't even suspend him from duty at this stage, we will have think long and hard, before going any further."

Once the phone call was over, Czerniak contacted Danny and Tony and told them to meet him in fifteen minutes on the beach at Pensarn.

He then told Rajni to leave what she was doing and to join him in his car and, without saying a word, he drove to a deserted section of beach frontage, to await the arrival of the other two team members.

"Look, I'm afraid we've pushed this case as far as we possibly can and so, for the sake of your careers, I want all three of you to go back to the hotel, pack your things and head back up to London, is that clear?" he said, as they walked along the shingle beach.

"Is that an order?" Rajni asked.

"Erm, yes, I suppose it is," he replied.

"Then, it's a shit one," she said, picking up a pebble to throw into the sea.

"Yeh, I agree," Tony added, "and to be honest Jack, it's one that you can't possibly expect us to follow."

"Well, I for one, won't be going anywhere, until that arrogant bastard gets what he deserves," Danny said, "Christ almighty, we can't let him get away with murder."

"Now listen here," Czerniak started to say, before he was bombarded with a chorus of "no, you listen to us," from all three.

"We're not going anywhere," Tony added, "well, not until we've finished the job we came to do in the first place."

"Well in that case, let's stop pissing about down here and get back to work," Czerniak said, his broad grin only too apparent.

Whilst Tony began the extremely tedious task, of trawling through bits of footage, which had been salvaged from the seized property store, CCTV hard drive, Czerniak headed off alone, to have a quiet, one to one conversation, with John Owen, head of SOCCO.

In the meantime, Danny and Rajni were also on a mission, only this one, involved a certain amount of subterfuge, as they were headed to Manchester, to secretly acquire CCTV footage, from the carpark of Bodelwyddan Hospital.

Believing that Chief Superintendent James Cooke, had been the uniformed officer, who on visiting Baris Dogan, had very cleverly, avoided all the internal security cameras, they hoped to find him outside in one of the dozen or so carparks.

Their need for secrecy, had arisen, after Danny and Tony had learnt, that Chief Superintendent Cooke, had been personally acquired, all of the hospitals' internal CCTV footage.

Claiming, that he was attempting to prove or, disprove, that Superintendent Griffiths had attempted to interfere with a vital witness in the case, the head of professional Standards, had demanded all of hospitals' CCTV from that day, insisting that any additional footage be destroyed.

However, he had overlooked the fact, that the hospital carparks, were privately-owned, and managed, by a Manchester based company, who used an ANPR system, to monitor the arrival and departure of all vehicles and, rigorously pursued anyone, who failed to pay their parking fee.

Already aware, that the head of Professional Standards had seized the hospitals CCTV footage, Harry Dobson, director of operations, was expecting a visit from the police.

Without confirming or denying, that they were part of Chief Superintendent Cooke's team, Danny, calmly flashed his police warrant card before explaining, that they were there to collect of copy of their ANPR and CCTV footage, from the day of the incident.

Having told Mr Dobson, that if there was nothing of value on the footage, their copy of it, would be destroyed, they handed him a receipt and left.

Once back in St Asaph and, with Danny keeping a watchful eye out for any unwanted visitors, especially DS Jarvis, Rajni began checking the CCTV, for any physical sightings of Cooke and, the ANPR recordings, hoping, at the very least, to see his car registration number.

Meanwhile, in an annexe building, set some distance, behind the police headquarters in

Colwyn Bay, Czerniak was sounding out John Owen, to see if he had any affiliations to the head of professional standards.

"To be perfectly honest with you," he replied quite bluntly, "as long as they don't interfere with me or my department anymore, I don't really care what they do."

"Do I take it, that hasn't always been the case?"

"Well, let's just say, that James Cooke, thought my predecessor, was only here to examine police officer's notebooks or, act as some sort of peeping Tom with his camera."

"Oh, I see, he thought he was some sort of one-man surveillance outfit."

"Yes, and that would still be the case, if I hadn't have told him bluntly, that we are a force resource and not here to serve one department."

"And what did he have to say about that?"

"None too happy, but there again, I wasn't brought in for me tact, I was hired to drag this force out of the nineteenth century and, to start embracing modern technology and methods, Christ, you should have seen some of the equipment I inherited," he said with a broad grin.

"What, out of the Ark?"

"Out of the Ark, I think some of it was used to build the bloody thing."

"Which will explain your comments about finding the fingerprints of certain senior officers at our crime scene the other day," Czerniak said subtly.

"Huh, seems they think, that anyone, over the rank of Superintendent doesn't have fingerprints," he replied, his face now contorted in a scowl.

"Anywhere of any importance?"

"Well, on your bloody stash point behind the painting for one."

"You are joking right?"

"No, found two sets actually in the stash point itself, one belonging to the Detective Chief Super and the other, to our head of professional standards, Christ, can you imagine if it ever got out, that two of the highest-ranking officers in the force are blundering about crime scenes, handling and touching what could be crucial evidence."

"Is it, common practice?"

"Do they come to every job, no thank god but, having said that, especially as now, Superintendent Griffiths is, what you might call, a person of interest in the case, Chief Super Cooke has been taking a keen interest in everything."

"Oh, you mean, because Mrs Griffiths was a victim of the shooting," Czerniak said, trying to sound as naïve as possible.

"Yes, exactly, and let's be fair, we all know or, at least, some of us suspect, that he was involved in some way, I mean, it stands to reason right."

"I couldn't comment," Czerniak said, tapping the side of his nose.

"Ah, least said eh!" John Owen said, with a knowing nod of his head.

"speaking of the shooting, were you involved at all, as I never saw your name on the witness list?"

"No, fortunately, it was the last day of my leave, so I missed all the fun and games," he replied.

"I take it by that, you mean, the bureaucratic mayhem?"

"Yes, and, with it being the wife of a serving police officer, on the night, apparently, anyone who was anyone, was trying their hardest to pull rank, you know, so that they could be the S.I.O. but in the end, James Cooke took control."

"Christ, don't tell me he left his prints everywhere?"

"Huh, no, and in fact, the lads who covered the job, told me, that despite there being signs of a search, they only found, those belonging to the two victims, oh, and of course, John Griffiths," he replied.

"When you say, signs of a search, I read that on the forensic report, that it mentioned glove marks, are we any closer to identifying what sort of gloves they were."

"Good question and, funnily enough, one I may have the answer to," he replied, picking up a manila coloured folder from his desk, "as we've just received this report from the forensic lab in Chorley, and they reckon, they were some sort of surgical gloves, you know, with a very fine, rubberised, almost smooth surface."

"A bit like the ones you and I would wear, if we were attending a crime scene?"

"Erm, yes, exactly," he replied awkwardly, "look, you're not suggesting, that one of my team contaminated the scene?"

"No, no, far from it," Czerniak said quickly, "I was merely trying to get my head around the type of gloves we're looking for and, from what you say, they could have been purchased in any supermarket."

"Erm, yes, yes, that's correct."

"I know, because of the involvement of Superintendent Griffiths, that the Home Office stepped in fairly early on in the investigation, but did your team manage to conduct a thorough search of the murder scene?"

"Well, I think is the correct answer is no, but, they did make a start of course, but then, you know, with Mr Griffiths being found at the scene, it was thought best, to bring in an outside team."

"Whose decision was that."

"I'm not too sure, but it would have no doubt, been in conjunction with the Home Office."

"So, was anything of any value found, you know, that might throw a light on a motive, I only ask because, we're still waiting for a SOCCO report?"

"Well no, because like I say, the rug was pulled from under our feet, long before a proper search could be carried out, so any report, will come from whoever Chief Superintendent Cooke called in."

Chapter 22.

The realisation, that a meticulous, fingertip search of the house, where Linda Griffiths and Garry Sunderland were shot and killed, had not been carried, came as a shock, to both Czerniak and John Owen.

So, to rectify matters, John Owen immediately mustered a team, who spent the next three days searching 32 Bryn Forydd Road and, it revealed, far more than Czerniak was expecting.

First of all, it showed, that contrary to popular belief, Mrs Griffiths and Sunderland may have been sharing the house, but they were very definitely, not co-habiting in the true sense of the word.

Because, in one bedroom, they found all of Gary Sunderland's clothing and personal effects and in another, which was very definitely the one used by Mrs Griffiths, all of her personal belongings.

It was, in the bedroom used by Mrs Griffiths that they found a small, pay as you go mobile phone, concealed deep inside the lining of the mattress, on the double bed.

Fortunately, as the mobile phones password, was 1234, Rajni was able to open it and, quickly see, that Mrs Griffiths had been using it to text the just one number and, for over twelve months.

"Shit, shit, shit," Rajni suddenly exclaimed, "it was Linda Griffiths, who killed Sunderland."

"She what?" Czerniak said, his voice slightly raised.

"Well, just listen to this," she said, before reading out a text, sent on the night Gary Sunderland was shot, "she says, 'I think I've killed him,' and someone texts back, 'what?' and she says, 'you never said it was loaded,' then the other person says, 'don't touch anything, I'm on my way.'"

"So, whoever received that message, is the person who supplied her with the gun and, on seeing what she'd written, has gone to the house and, presumably shot her to cover his or her tracks."

"Yeh, because they also sent a text to her a few minutes later, telling her to hide anything which might incriminate them."

"Which is probably why, she stuffed the phone inside the mattress."

"Hang on a minute, whoever she was texting, it looks like, she'd been seeing them, since early last year," Rajni said as she started to scroll back, through the older text messages.

"Any idea who it was?" Czerniak asked.

"No, but it definitely wasn't Gary Sunderland, look," she replied, showing a message to Czerniak, "see, she's saying, 'G out tonight with D and staying over'."

"What about her most recent messages, anything there?"

"Erm, bloody hell, that's interesting," Rajni replied, whilst reading another text message, "it's from the Tuesday before she was killed and, she's saying 'big fight tonight, G says, he knows who you are."

"Is there a reply?"

"Yeh, they've written, 'how?' and she's texted back, 'think he followed me to Northop last week, says deal is off, what shall we do?' so, what do you think, it's another man and he's married or something and afraid of his wife finding out."

"Yeh, something like that, so, has he replied?"

"Later that night, he's texted, asking, 'is our insurance policy safe,' and she replied, 'yes, but he's still not happy,' then nothing, until following morning, when she texts to say 'very worried, he's acting odd and policy missing,' do you think the insurance policy their talking about, could be that tape-recording John Griffiths told you about?"

"I'd say so and, if I'm right, was the reason why the garage was broken into the night before the killings," Czerniak said, looking pensive, "so, go on, what does she say next?"

"Kicking off again, says he's going to go and see John," Rajni replied, having read the next text message.

"Bloody hell, what did he have to say about that?"

"7, in College Lane."

"Shit, so they met up, Wednesday night, which means, we've no idea what was said."

"No, but according to her next text, she says that Sunderland was still mad and, after finding out about the break in, told her he's afraid and, is taking the recording and leaving the country," Rajni replied, before suddenly going silent, "so, presumably, after she kills kill him, the boyfriend comes around and they search for the tape recording, but, if he was leaving with it, why didn't they find it?"

"Good question and one, I think your father, unwittingly, gave me the answer to."

As Rajni typed out a transcript of the text messages, Czerniak contacted George Hanson in the Home office, to ask for permission, to interview, Chief Superintendent Cooke.

Meanwhile, Danny and Tony headed over to the seized property store, to collect the holdall which had been found in the rear of Gary Sunderland's car.

The substantial looking holdall, made of thick, heavy duty leather, still contained some items of clothing, but other than that, it looked to be empty.

"Bloody heavy old thing," Tony remarked as he placed it on Czerniak's desk.

"I take it, it's been to forensics?" Czerniak asked.

"Yeh, looks like it's done the rounds in the last week or so, as it's only just come back from professional standards."

"Has it really?" Czerniak asked, with the glimmer of a smile crossing his face.

"That was, a Mr Hanson, from the Home Office," Rajni said, as she put the phone down, "seems your interview with Chief Superintendent Cooke, is due to take place at eleven tomorrow morning."

"Did he say who the senior officer is going to be?"

"Yes, Mr Meres, the Chief Constable from Cheshire."

"Right, in that case, I want all three of you out collecting CCTV footage."

"Anywhere in particular," Rajni asked cheekily.

"Well, for one thing, see what you can dig up from around the murder scene, before and after the times, the shootings are alleged to have taken place."

"Alleged?" Tony asked.

"Yeh, because up until now, we've been working on the assumption that John Griffiths shot them, at around midnight, but what if it took place much earlier."

"And after midnight?" Tony queried.

"Because I'd like to know for sure, who arrived on the scene after it was reported and, from what direction."

"Hmm, you've got a bloody devious mind boss," Tony said with a chuckle.

"What about the College Road, mentioned in the text messages?" Rajni asked.

"Do we know where it is?"

"Erm, I've looked on Google Maps and there are two in the area," she replied.

"Well, best get your skates on then," he said clapping his hands loudly, "come on, chop, chop the bloody clock is ticking.

Then, at five minutes to eleven, the following morning and, flanked by his solicitor, Chief Superintendent Cooke arrived at St Asaph police station.

"I'm here to see Detective Inspector Czerniak," he said, in a very terse manner, as he addressed the custody sergeant.

"Yes sir, this way," the custody sergeant said as he directed them along the narrow corridor.

After the initial introduction had been carried out and Czerniak had switched on the recording device, he read out the caution, before looking the Chief Superintendent in the eyes and asking him, if he fully understood his legal rights.

The look of animosity, in Chief Superintendent Cooke's eyes, as he glowered back across the desk was all too apparent and caused, Chief Constable Meres to move uncomfortably in his seat.

"Can I begin, by asking, how long you have known Superintendent John Griffiths?"

"Erm, I couldn't say for sure, but a number of years," he replied as vaguely as possible.

"I believe, whilst you were the DCI in Llandudno, he became DI in Abergele, is that correct?"

"Is this really necessary," he replied, "as it's a point of record, where each of us have served and, the dates we served there."

"I am merely trying to show, for the benefit of this recording, which has no access to police personnel files, that for a period of time you were a senior officer, with responsibility for

Abergele C.I.D and ultimately, you would have been in a position to issue orders to, the then, DI Griffiths."

"Yes, if that makes you happy."

"Thank you," Czerniak replied, ignoring the glare from Cooke, "now then, can I take you to the early hours of Saturday, the Fourth of April this year and ask, at what stage were you informed of the double shooting at 32, Forydd road in Rhyl?"

"Erm, well, obviously, because one of the victims, was the wife of a serving, senior officer, who was also at the scene, it was immediately flagged up to me."

"And did you go directly to the scene?"

"Yes," he replied, again his impatience showing, "look, once again you are repeating things which are a matter of record, so can you please, get to the reason you have humiliated me by dragging me here today."

"What time did you arrive at the scene?" Czerniak asked, ignoring Cooke and his comments.

"I have no idea, about three, maybe half past, you'd have to check with the crime scene log."

"I did," Czerniak replied, "and, it was two fifteen, in fact, you arrived there, only half an hour after the ops room had notified you."

"Is that a question or a statement?"

"To my knowledge, you live in Rhos on Sea and, even in the early hours of the morning, you would be hard pressed to travel to Rhyl and the scene of the shootings, in half an hour."

"Excuse me, Chief Constable Meres, is there a point to any of this, as so far, D/I Czerniak is just making statements and not asking my client questions of any relevance?" the solicitor suddenly said.

"I think, D/I Czerniak is making a valid point," Mr Meres said quietly. "So, answer the question, where were you, when you received the telephone call from your operations room?"

"Erm, I'd rather not answer that question at this time, as for one thing, it is a private matter, which has no relevance to this case."

"Are you saying, you were not at home, when you received the phone call."

"If you don't mind, I would like a private word with my solicitor."

Chapter 23.

When they returned to the interview room, a rather steely faced Chief Superintendent sat in silence, whilst his solicitor read out a short, prepared statement.

"My client, wishes to assist this enquiry in the best way he can and, to that end, he would like to divulge a rather embarrassing personal fact, which is, that for the last couple of months he has been conducting an extra-marital affair with a married woman and, in order to save her marriage, erm, and of course his own, he will not be supplying her name at this time."

"So, are you saying, that at the time you received the phone call from ops room, notifying you of the double murder, you were with another person?"

"yes."

"Thank you, so, now that we've cleared up that little anomaly, we can perhaps move on," Czerniak said with a faint smile, designed to make Cooke, think he had nothing else of significance to ask him, "so, can you tell me who was at the scene when you arrived?"

"Erm, let me see," he replied, now that a certain amount of former arrogance and confidence had been restored, "ah yes, the two, first responders, John Griffiths of course and the paramedics, who I believe had only just arrived."

"And what did you do?"

"Do, I went inside of course, after all, a double murder had just been reported."

"And the two, uniformed first responders where were they."

"Erm, I believe, I told them to guard the perimeter, you know, to prevent any contamination of the crime scene."

"And where was John Griffiths at this time?"

"Erm, he was sat in the hallway, next to Sunderland's body."

"Did you speak to him, or ask what had happened?"

"Yes, but he was totally incoherent and not making much sense."

"So, what did you do next?"

"I, erm, well, after a quick look in the kitchen, you know, at the body of Mrs Griffiths, I went upstairs and checked for signs of an intruder."

"Very commendable, considering you were unarmed."

"I'm sorry, are you making fun of me?" he asked angrily.

"No, far from it, because, after all, you had just arrived at the scene of a double shooting and, as there was a strong possibility, that the offenders were still on the premises, I think it was a very courageous thing to do."

"Erm, yes, erm, thank you."

"Not at all," Czerniak said, nodding his head, "tell me, Chief Superintendent, what were you wearing at the time."

"I'm sorry, what does it matter what I was wearing, two people had just been shot."

"No, you miss understand me, what I'm referring to, is what protection against cross contamination of the scene were you wearing."

"Hmm, yes, I see what you mean," he replied, now a little calmer, "erm, well, rubber gloves and over shoes of course and, a standard, white, paper suit."

"Which presumably, you always keep in your private car, just in case you're called to a crime scene out of hours?"

"Yes, well, in our force at least, it's standard practice for all senior officers to carry a forensic set in their car."

"So, what you're saying, is, despite the fact that you thought the offenders might still be on the scene, you took the time, to put on a pair of overshoes, rubber gloves and, a white paper suit."

"Christ man, do I have to spell everything out to you, yes, like I say, it's standard practice to carry them and, I might add, to wear them when visiting a crime scene."

"Is it, then, perhaps you can explain, why you never wore any of those things when you visited the home of Baris Dogan, after he was shot with the same gun, that killed those two people?"

"I beg your pardon, I think you'll find, that you are very much mistaken."

"I'm afraid not, because, for one thing, if you cast your mind back to that day Chief Superintendent, I was in that house when you barged in and another, you left your fingerprints at several crucial areas around that crime scene."

"So, what's your point?"

"My point is, why did you spend, what, five minutes, donning protective clothing before entering a crime scene, where you suspected, that the offenders were still on the premises and yet, not bother with any protective clothing, when attending one, when the offender was long gone."

"Yet again sergeant, you are making pointless remarks, so, have you any real questions to put to me, as I do have quite a busy schedule today."

"So, one of my team, tells me that your office has been examining the leather holdall which was found in the boot of Gary Sunderland's car, can you tell me why?" Czerniak asked, whilst ignoring the gibe.

"Well, I would have thought, that was obvious," he replied sarcastically.

"Not really no, so, could you please answer the question."

"Good god man, I am the head of the force Professional Standards department and, if I'm not very much mistaken, your chief suspect in a double murder, is, Superintendent John Griffiths, a serving police officer, so yes, I am going to dig and delve, in order to get to the bottom of this because, from what I've seen of your slipshod methods so far, I think it's highly unlikely that you will ever solve this case."

"So, you've examined the leather holdall, did you find anything to incriminate either Superintendent Griffiths or anyone else?"

"Erm, well, not exactly."

"It's a simple question Chief Superintendent, did you find anything, yes or no?"

"No."

"Hmm, tell me, what do you know about Hawala banks?"

"For goodness sake, do I have to sit here and listen to any more of this this idiot's drivel?"

"What do you know about Hawala banks?" Czerniak repeated, ignoring the Cooke's remarks.

"Nothing, why, is it important?"

"Yes, if you wish to know the relevance of this holdall and why, it plays such a pivotal role in this case," Czerniak said as he lifted the leather holdall out of the plastic exhibit bag. "You see, along with his partner, Mr Dogan,

Gary Sunderland ran what is known as a Hawala bank and, for those who are not acquainted with the name, it's an age-old system for transferring large amounts of money around the world. Normally used by elderly and middle aged, Asian and Middle Eastern business men, it allows them to avoid the usual bureaucratic scrutiny that normal banks now insist on."

"But I still don't see how this, impacts on my interest in the holdall."

"Well, let me explain how it works," Czerniak said, ignoring the Chief Superintendents apparent lack of interest in the bag, "So, you have a man, here in North Wales who wishes to transfer twenty thousand pounds, to his family, in say, Istanbul. So, he takes the money to his local Hawala bank, who have contacts with a similar establishment in Istanbul and, without any money actually leaving the UK at that time, it's transferred, in local currency, to the waiting family member."

"Yes, that's all very interesting I'm sure, but how does that concern me and why, I'm listening to you drone on, about something of absolutely no value in this case."

"Well, let me explain, you see, at some stage, especially when the flow of money has only been in one direction, a physical transfer has to take place, but, as we all know, because of money laundering laws, no one can take more than ten thousand pounds out of the country, well, not without answering a whole raft of awkward questions," Czerniak said, as he opened the holdall, "So, in certain quarters of the middle east, a small, but exclusive cottage industry was set up to manufacture holdalls, just like this one, each one, with a secret compartment, lined with wafer thin strips of lead to shield its contents from airport scanners."

While the Chief Constable and the solicitor stood to look inside the holdall, Chief Superintendent Cooke sat back, his face contorted in shock and horror.

"You see, if he had lived, Mr Sunderland or, should I say, Georgio Cartulary, as that was his real name, was due to fly to Istanbul on that Saturday with, what I believe, was his escape money, some twenty thousand pounds, which incidentally, we found hidden inside his holdall, together, with this," Czerniak said, holding up a small, Dictaphone tape. "Tell me Chief Superintendent Cooke, would you like to tell the others in the room what is on this tape, or shall I."

"Oh, do spare us the amateur theatricals Inspector and get on with this charade," Cooke replied with an arrogant shrug of his shoulders.

"Tell me, how long had you and Mrs Linda Griffiths been in a relationship?" Czerniak asked.

"Do what?" Cooke replied, his face contorted and full of anger, "how dare you besmirch the memory of that poor woman with such ridiculous allegations."

"Did it start, when she came to you and told you what she'd found in her husband's belongings?"

"Good god Chief Constable are you just going to sit there while this idiot makes such slanderous remarks?" he demanded.

"Did she tell you, that she knew what you'd done," Czerniak asked, as he continued to ignore the Chief Superintendent, "and, did she suggest joining forces to extract money from John Griffiths?"

"This is ridiculous and, as I'm here voluntarily and, have not so far, been charged with any offences, I intend leaving," he said as he stood to leave.

"Now then, bearing in mind, that my team have recovered CCTV footage from a number of locations, I'll ask you, what went through your mind, when Linda Griffiths sent you a text message, telling you that she'd killed Gary Sunderland?"

"What did you just say?" Cooke replied, as he slumped back into his seat.

"Oh, yes, didn't I mention, that we also recovered the burner phone Mrs Griffiths had been using to contact you for the last twelve months," Czerniak said, as he held the small mobile phone up for Cooke to see, "you know, the one you messaged her on, to ask if she'd found the insurance policy and then, arranged to meet her in College Road."

"Why, I mean, you have no proof, you have absolutely no proof, it was me," he replied, his shoulders suddenly sagging.

"Tell me, Chief Superintendent Cooke, do you recognise this man, who seems to be handing a package of some description to Linda

Griffiths," he asked, showing a still photograph, taken from the CCTV in College Road.

"No comment."

"What were you giving her?"

"No comment."

"Was it a handgun and silencer?"

"No comment."

"His insurance policy, against you, is what John Griffiths called this didn't he," Czerniak said, as he held up the Dictaphone tape, "because he'd taped you, giving him a direct order, to task an informant, with finding some evidence, which would allow you, to convict an innocent man of rape, events, which eventually led, to that innocent man being killed and the informant, being sent to prison for manslaughter."

"Poppycock, I mean, how can anyone possibly prove it was me."

"I'm afraid, we have a signed statement from Superintendent John Griffiths, who identifies you as the senior officer who instructed him to send an informant, to, and I quote, 'dig up whatever dirt he can because, I don't care if he's done it or not, that bastard Finnegan is going down for this'," Czerniak said, reading from the written statement, "he also goes on to say, that just prior to the two killings, you once again gave him a direct order, when you instructed him to task that very same informant, with breaking into the car showroom, run by Gary Sunderland."

"Utter lies, the man is delusional, surely it's him who should be here answering these questions."

"So, bearing in mind, that we have recovered CCTV of you, heading to the murder scene, at ten o'clock that night, I'll ask you again, what did you think, when Mrs Griffiths informed you, via that text message, that she'd killed Gary Sunderland."

"Stupid bitch!" he replied quietly, "why she had to involve him in the first place I'll never know."

"Are you talking about Gary Sunderland?"

"Sunderland, Cartulary, whatever his bloody name was, he was nothing more than an annoyance from the outset, always getting in the way and asking questions."

"Until he found out about you?"

"Yes, I suppose so, you see, what you must understand, that Linda and I, well, we go way back, in fact, she was the reason my first marriage failed," he said, looking dejected, "then, when she married John Griffiths, I thought she might be willing to help recover the tape."

"So, she got him drunk and got him to reveal it's whereabouts."

"Yes, something like that, but it was in his safe and, she couldn't get her hands on it."

"Is that why Sunderland was recruited?"

"He was supposed to go to the house to collect a cash payment for a car and, when the safe was open, somehow grab the tape, which he did, but then kept it to make sure he got his cut."

"But then, being the greedy bastard, he was, he wanted a far bigger cut, especially when he discovered how much money John Griffiths had in the bank."

"You have it in one, so, we arranged for Linda to move in with him and, everything seemed to be going to plan, until he followed her to our meeting place and, having heard the tape, and worked out who I was, thought I might, somehow double cross him."

"Which is why, you gave Linda the gun in College Road?"

"She was only supposed to frighten him with it for Christ sake, not bloody shoot him."

"My question to you now, is, why did you shoot her?"

"Because, she'd become hysterical and, even before I got there, she'd already decide to confess everything to John."

"So, you shot her?"

"Yes, but the first shot was only meant to shut her up, but she moved and it hit her in the stomach, then when she went for me and tried to grab the gun, I had no other choice."

"And Dogan?"

"Another, ineffectual lying bastard," he replied angrily, "I wanted Hinchcliffe to break in there and plant the gun, but he said he didn't want any part of it."

"So, what, you handcuffed him and then, gave him an overdose."

"His type, are a bloody waste of space anyway, do you know, he'd never done an honest day's work in his entire life, so yes, I sent him on his way as after all, it was only a matter of time."

Chapter 24.

Having been charged with the murders of Linda Griffiths and Jimmy Hinchcliffe and the attempted murder of Baris Dogan, a still defiant and arrogant James Cooke was put before a court, who, much to the disgraced Chief Superintendent's surprise, remanded him in custody.

They may have got their man, but the team still had a long slog ahead and, if they were going prove the case against Cooke, they had to ensure, that every last detail was dealt with correctly and, that every I was dotted and ever t crossed.

Amongst the lower ranks within the Welsh force, there was very little sympathy for a man, who many considered to be a bully who, on many occasions, had gone out of his way to hound some hapless bobby out of the job, on charges, which in many ways, deserved no more than a tap on the wrist.

However, amongst the upper echelons of the force, Czerniak noticed there were signs, that the more senior officers, who had served alongside Cooke, were now, very definitely closing ranks.

It was, as he recorded a long formal statement from John Griffiths that Czerniak learnt, that far from feeling sympathy for Cooke, certain senior officers feared what secrets he may be willing to disclose in order to get a lighter sentence.

"How likely is that?" Czerniak asked, as they shared a cup of coffee.

"Well, as you know, he's a cunning bastard and, has a wealth of knowledge about each every one of them and, more to the point, their individual dalliances and foibles shall we say."

"So, you think he's been storing up the black he has on everyone just for such an occasion as this?"

"There have been several occasions in the past, when, having sailed too close to the wind, everyone thought, that at the very least, he'd be demoted, but, as per usual he ended up, coming out of it smelling of roses."

"In that case, I'll have to be doubly sure that the bastard doesn't talk his way out of this one then," Czerniak said with a wry smile.

"Just watch your back lad, that's all I'm saying, because they'll be lining up, to do his bidding."

With the warning well and truly noted, Czerniak informed his small team and told them, that under no circumstances should they discuss the case with anyone.

Then, only days later, Superintendent Glyn Pritchard, the new acting head of the force Professional Standards department made a surprise visit to the office.

After a long preamble, about how the force's reputation had been tarnished by, as he put it, this unfortunate scandal, Superintendent Pritchard asked, how confident Czerniak was of getting a conviction.

"Well, bearing in mind, that in interview, Cooke admitted the offences, I would say pretty strong sir," he replied politely.

"Hmm, yes, listen, I don't wish to be picky, but as the evidence hasn't even been put before a court yet, I really think, that Chief Superintendent Cooke should be given all due courtesy, especially when referring to him by name, don't you think, acting Inspector."

"As you wish sir," Czerniak replied, as he realised that the witch hunt had begun.

For the remaining half hour of his visit, as he tried to probe deeper into the case and more crucially, what other evidence the team had amassed, Superintendent Pritchard only received vague and very guarded answers from Czerniak and, frustrated by his lack of progress, demanded to see a copy of the prosecution file, before it was sent to the Crown Prosecution Service.

Fearing, that Superintendent Pritchard might try and somehow sabotage his case file, Czerniak made contact, with George Hanson at the Home Office.

It was, with the full backing of the Home Office that, two weeks, the completed prosecution file was presented to the lead lawyer at the CPS who, had already been briefed by George Hanson.

As tempers flared in the Professional Standards office, Czerniak and, his small team, cleared their incident room.

"I can't wait to get home and have one of my mum's meals," Rajni said, as she placed the last box of documents in the back of the car.

"Well, if it's a curry, you can count me in," Tony called out as he climbed into the driver's seat of the other vehicle, "no offence to Wales, but you can't get a decent one anywhere up here."

"Huh, yeh, I'll second that," Danny added, "especially after that awful one I had the other week, Christ I'm still running to the bog even now."

"Right, lets get this show on the road," Czerniak called out as he slipped into the passenger's seat next to Rajni.

Printed in Dunstable, United Kingdom